MATCH MADE IN SEVILLE

MICHELE RENAE

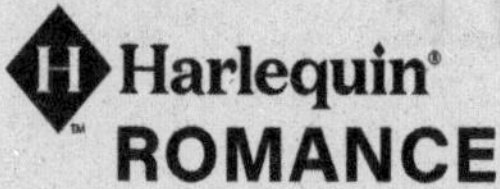

Recycling programs for this product may not exist in your area.

ISBN-13: 978-1-335-47084-3

Match Made in Seville

For questions and comments about the quality of this book, please contact us at CustomerService@Harlequin.com.

Harlequin Enterprises ULC
22 Adelaide St. West, 41st Floor
Toronto, Ontario M5H 4E3, Canada
www.Harlequin.com

HarperCollins Publishers
Macken House, 39/40 Mayor Street Upp
Dublin 1, D01 C9W8, Ireland
www.HarperCollins.com

Printed in U.S.A.

1 2 3 4 5 6 7 8 9 10 HDC 28 27 26 25

A dazzling new Harlequin Romance duet.

Cinderellas in Seville

Once upon a Spanish romance…

CEOs Mateo and Valentino's success has exceeded their wildest dreams. Over the past decade, they've taken the VR gaming world by storm to honor their late friend Pablo after his tragically young death. Romantic relationships, on the other hand, had to take a back seat…

Only now, thanks to the transformative presence of two enchanting women, it's all they can think about. And they're about to discover that love is much more complex than code. It's a game they must play to win!

In *CEO's Spanish Fling*
by Justine Lewis

Teo and Pablo's ex, Cara, never liked each other. But now she's in Seville, she needs his help and he's the only one she can turn to—sparking an attraction between them that sets his well-ordered life aflame!

In *Match Made in Seville*
by Michele Renae

Workaholic Val enlists the help of an elite matchmaking service to find a wife—only to find himself entranced by a woman who is his polar opposite: his perfectionist dating consultant, Amber. No algorithm in the world can predict the outcome of their unforeseen connection!

Both available now!

Michele Renae is the pseudonym for award-winning author Michele Hauf. She has published over ninety novels in historical, paranormal, and contemporary romance and fantasy, as well as written action/adventure as Alex Archer. Instead of "writing what she knows," she prefers to write "what she would love to know and do" (and yes, that includes being a jewel thief and/or a brain surgeon).

You can email Michele at toastfaery@gmail.com.
Instagram: @MicheleHauf
Pinterest: @ToastFaery

Books by Michele Renae

Harlequin Romance

If the Fairy Tale Fits...

Cinderella's Billion-Dollar Invitation

A White Christmas in Whistler

Their Midnight Mistletoe Kiss

Art of Being a Billionaire

Faking It with the Boss
Billion-Dollar Nights in the Castle
Jet-Set Nights with Her Enemy

Fairy Tales in Maine

Cinderella's One-Night Surprise

Consequence of Their Parisian Night
Two Week Temptation in Paradise
Reunion with Her Highland Rival

Visit the Author Profile page at Harlequin.com.

CHAPTER ONE

THE VASQUEZ ESTATE, nestled in Seville's barrio de Santa Cruz, boasted an Instagram-worthy lush courtyard. Amber Martin strolled over the tiles curving along the shaded path. Birds chirped. Sweet orange blossoms bursting on the half-dozen potted trees perfumed her senses as she inhaled. Water bubbling in the center fountain tugged a rare smile onto her lips.

Had she stepped into a dream?

Until today, her passport had only marked France and the US. This was her first official assignment as a lifestyle consultant for Lux Love, the elite dating servicc that guaranteed an ultimate love match for the rich and famous. Yes, even the seemingly privileged needed help finding a lifelong companion.

Amber's job involved assessing the client's lifestyle from living environment, personality, hobbies, communication and so much more. Their bespoke matchmaking never paired two people who did not match at less than 90 percent.

It was a big task to undertake, but Amber was ready. It had been years since she'd lost her job as a paralegal because AI had made her position obsolete. Since then, she'd worked for a few small boutiques back in Minnesota, her home state, but hoped to someday utilize her research and communications degrees.

Last year she'd gotten the job as an assistant to an assistant to Colette Bellerose, international style icon, and founder and CEO of Lux Love. In Paris! Thank you, Aunt Judy, who had known Colette and mentioned Amber's desire to learn in a foreign country. Sure, at the time, Amber hadn't an interest in matchmaking, but no sane woman would refuse a job in Paris. Over the past year doing research and data entry for Colette, Amber had watched, trained and prepared for when she would be given her first client.

Don't let Lux Love down, Colette had said over the phone while Amber had been boarding a red-eye to Paris. When she'd heard about the job, she'd been in Minnesota visiting her dad. It had been too late to change her flight, so she'd flown to Paris-Charles de Gaulle, then immediately hopped a flight to Seville. It was now seven in the evening, Spanish time. The entire day had been spent in the air and in TSA check lines. In total she'd been awake for—no. Doing the math would only depress her. She'd considered calling and arranging to meet Senor Vasquez tomorrow after she slept off the jet lag but she didn't want the client's first impression of her to be canceling an appointment. She could push through the exhaustion for a brief introductory meeting.

The last thing Colette had warned her before boarding was: *Don't fall in love with the client.*

Amber muttered now as she approached the front doorway of the client's villa. "Who does she think I am? I won't fall in love. I don't *do* love. Love is…"

For everybody else. She'd never met a man who could challenge her intellectually or hold her interest for more than a day or two. And with her parents' divorce only three years in the past, she was still clinging to the realization that love couldn't last.

As well, self-aware as she tried to be, she knew her emotional IQ needed tending. And that actually made her perfect for the job of matchmaker. She was able to stand aside and observe the client's life, make notes, suggest ways to improve his or her profile and gain a match. All without becoming emotionally involved. She'd ace this job.

With an adjusting tug to her red Anne Klein suit—she'd had her colors done; it was her power color—and gripping her CHANEL purse tightly, which she'd be paying off on her credit card for years!, she rapped the guitar-shaped brass door knocker.

The owner, Valentino Vasquez, was not a musician that she knew of. There had been some mention of flamenco dance in his preliminary survey. Trying to get some sleep during the flight to Paris so she could be attentive and alert for her first big job had failed. She could never sleep on a plane. But it had given her time to study Vasquez's profile. The thirty-two-year-old Spanish native was a billionaire CEO—along with his partner, Mateo Ortiz—of the virtual reality gaming corporation, Verdadero. That meant *truth*, or *real*. Valentino was the coding genius of the pair. He'd called Lux Love two days ago requesting a match, which had set the vetting process into motion.

The comment section regarding his reason for seeking a match had been blank. Not an issue. Amber would learn everything about the man and get to know him better than any family member could.

The door opened to reveal a short woman of indeterminate age. A gush of rose perfume exuded from her body. Silver streaks highlighted her pulled-back black hair. Rounded shoulders and an apron over a plain brown dress. A housekeeper or chef? The woman cast her gaze over all five feet eight inches—in heels—of Amber but she didn't say anything.

"Hola, I'm with the agency," Amber said in Spanish. "Senor Vasquez is expecting me. I'm Amber Martin."

And…that was about as much Spanish as she could wield conversationally.

With only the one year of middle school Spanish under her belt, Lord help her if she was to converse with the client in Spanish.

"*Sí,* Emmer."

"Uh… Amber." A glance to the side revealed an open closet spewing a tumble of shoes, coats and outer gear. Amber began mental note-taking. Messes like that screamed disinterest or neglect. Or possibly the need for a cleaning person.

"*Sí,* come this way." The woman spoke rapid Spanish. "Senor Vasquez is at office. I show you to the work."

Senor Vasquez was still at work? She'd made an appointment via text for this evening; had overtipped the cab driver to step on the gas. Granted, it was an unusual time of day to meet, but Vasquez had texted it would be perfect. She could meet him, give him a rundown of what to expect and then retire to the hotel, where she'd had her luggage sent, and crash.

Amber followed dutifully as the maid led her through the house, across an inner courtyard open to the sky that mirrored the outer courtyard and up a stairway. She was no architectural expert, but this place screamed traditional Spanish influence with the cream-painted walls and tiled columns. Bright tiles on the floors and walls. Lots of plants in huge terra-cotta pots. And an airy openness that made her heart sigh. If she had the money for a place this grand, she would certainly indulge herself.

Someday she would.

The housekeeper directed her to walk through a door. "It is inside." The woman's phone buzzed in a hip pocket, which she patted. "I will leave you. I have my stories."

"Gracias—" Amber flinched as the door closed in her face. Really? "Not the friendliest."

Making friends with the staff wasn't necessary. Not yet. The housekeeper could provide insight into Senor Vasquez's life. She'd talk with her, and any other staff, only with the client's permission.

Strolling down a short hallway, she walked into… "A closet?"

Three times the size of her bedroom in the 9th arrondissement flat, which she shared with two other Lux Love consultants. It looked like a showroom, or a designer clothing shop. Well lit with dark woods and suede-lined walls. Three of the walls were shelved, racked and…impossibly messy. A vanity with a mirror and scattered grooming products occupied one wall. In the center of the room stood a marble-topped counter where a few watches had been laid out on a black velvet cloth. Beside that were tossed unmatched socks and…she averted her gaze from the boxer shorts.

Yes, she'd been briefed that her role in vetting the client could become intimate, in a manner. She would need to learn everything about Senor Vasquez's life. That included ticking off items regarding his sexual preferences.

Amber turned, taking in the clothing, which seemed a mix of expensive suits—thankfully, hung—and T-shirts and sweatpants. A little odd the housekeeper had taken her here to begin her work. Perhaps it was a passive-aggressive means to showing Amber where the worst problem was?

Her shoulders tightened as taut as violin strings at the sight of clothing piled here and there, the leather shoes scattered, the— "That silk tie must be worth a fortune."

Plucking up the crumpled pink silk, she smoothed it out before hanging it among many others displayed on a wall. The man needed a closet cleanup. She would note that on her to-do list. But why didn't the housekeeper take care of his things?

"Weird."

Messiness was not a deal-breaker, but this sort of disarray usually came from a lifelong habit.

She'd do her best to gently but firmly guide him toward a tidier home. No woman wanted to marry a little boy who expected her to clean up after him.

But *she* also had to remember that one person's mess was another person's comfort. And messy people often matched to one another. Lux Love never tried to match an exact replica to the client. And truly, opposites never paired well. A happy medium always proved best.

If Vasquez wasn't home, she didn't want to start sorting through his things without his permission. She'd text him; possibly he was on his way home. Pulling her phone from her purse, she strode back to the door and—it didn't open.

"Locked?" She tried again. The knob twisted but didn't click open. "Did she purposely…?"

No. The housekeeper had no motivation to lock Amber in. It must have accidentally locked. A muscle twinged across her shoulders. This day had been too long.

Returning to the closet, Amber realized she wasn't hot from the stifling confines—the AC was on and it felt rather nice in here. But rather… she was so tired.

She tapped the phone screen but it remained dark. Out of charge? Seriously?

She'd had her bags—with the phone charger inside—sent to the hotel. Eying the outlets set around the center table, she wondered if there was a phone charger in one of the drawers. After a quick check, she didn't find any.

A glance to the mirror on the opposite wall displayed a frustrated, tired woman who was trying to hold it together on her first big job. "This has to go well," she said to her weary reflection.

Failure never earned the gold star.

Plopping on to an ultracomfy chaise longue before a narrow window that overlooked the inner courtyard, Amber shook her head. She could imagine Colette shaking her perfectly coiffed head and muttering how she should have sent Chantelle instead.

Amber would not tell her boss about this little misstep. Senor Vasquez would find her soon enough, if the housekeeper didn't come looking for her before that.

Life was all about achieving and moving forward. One step higher on the career ladder. One more credit card bill paid. Challenge was what nudged her out of bed in the morning. She could do this. And she would.

A yawn preceded a sigh, and then…

Val Vasquez strolled through the kitchen and grabbed an electrolyte drink from the fridge. His housekeeper kept all the necessities in stock. She knew he liked to jog home from work. Even if it was after dark.

He tilted back the lemon-flavored drink in a long swallow, then swiped the back of his hand across his mouth. Leaving the lights off, he sprinted up the inner courtyard stairs. The lush orange blossoms scented his house with a honey-citrus perfume.

Once in his bedroom, he tossed his sweaty shirt to the floor and aimed for the bathroom. A cool shower was in order.

Five minutes later, he wrapped a towel around his hips and entered the digital code on the closet door. He kept valuables inside so security was necessary. He entered the closet to grab a pair of linen sleep pants. Why were the lights on? Had they been left on since morning?

"Whatever." He veered toward the pants section.

But what was that? He spied something on the chaise before the window that overlooked the courtyard. Had Maria let in Emmer, the watch repairman? It was late to still be here. And he was…sleeping?

Who would take a nap while working? He glanced to the other door that opened to the hallway. The knob always jammed; something else for security to fix.

Wandering over, he deftly avoided a heap of dirty clothes with a jump to the side. He leaned over the chaise to jostle Emmer awake but retracted his hand before he could touch.

"A woman?"

CHAPTER TWO

SOMETHING NUDGED AMBER AWAKE. She shook her head. Winced at a kink in her neck. Opened her eyes.

A man leaned over her. He swept his fingers through his hair. Rich, curly dark hair that fell over one deep brown eye. Light glinted like jewels in his soft irises. So captivating. Did she…know him?

Wait. Was she—had she been sleeping? And a strange man loomed over her.

Amber startled upright on the chaise, swinging her feet to the floor. Where was she? *Closet.* She'd been…yes, locked inside. Had sat down because… *Jet lag.* And the man…was he…he wore but a towel!

"Oh no. I, uh…was not sleeping. I, uh, Senor Vasquez?"

"In the flesh."

He splayed out his arms as if to say *Look all you like*. Amber tried desperately not to, but… *abs*. Many rows of abs. So hard. And tight. She narrowed her gaze and started to count—

"You are not Emmer Ruiz."

Emmer? Where had she heard that name? Ah. "No, it's *Amber.* Amber Martin. I don't know any Emmer."

"Emmer is the name of the watch repairman that I assume Maria thought she let into this room. But the watches haven't been touched. And you are a sleeping beauty."

"I'm so sorry." Jumping to stand, she stepped near the window, hand fluttering nervously to her chest. A yawn was unpreventable. How long had she slept? "I was locked in. I wanted to call your maid to let me out but my phone is dead. I'm Amber, with Lux Love. We had an appointment this evening?"

"I thought that appointment was tomorrow?"

"I just spoke to you last night—er…" What time was it? "I'm…sorry, I don't think I made a mistake in the day…"

He tapped the watch on his wrist. "I never get things on my calendar. I think about it and then… eh. I got you switched around in my head with the watch repairman. Sorry."

"That's…" So not acceptable for his dating future. She could not abide a disorganized man.

Oh yeah, Amber? You're not here to vet him for yourself.

Right. She clutched her purse to her stomach. "We all forget on occasion, Senor Vasquez.

And it was a last-minute appointment. I didn't mean to nap in your home, but when I couldn't get out..."

"Not your fault. That knob needs to be fixed. And I always lock the other door on the bedroom side." He gestured to the mirror hung on the wall, which acted as an illusion that did not scream *Door right here!*

"I hadn't noticed that door. Anyway, once I sat down...jet lag attacked. I've been traveling all day. Started in Minnesota."

"That's a long haul. I did assume you were American from your accent."

Nodding, she put a palm over her mouth as she yawned again. Seriously. She just needed a real bed and some uninterrupted sleep. "My flight, which I hadn't had time to change, took me to Paris, and then here. It's been a whirlwind, to say the least."

"Don't worry about it, Senorita Martin." He wandered around the center console and shoved a random pile of boxer shorts to the floor. Cast her a glance. Like he thought she'd *not* seen that?

"Uh..." Her eyes kept landing on his impossible abs. *Likes to work out* would definitely be noted on his profile. Amber rubbed a hand along the back of her neck. "I know this is a very strange beginning..."

His biceps flexed as he waved his arms back

and forth, meeting before his hips in a fist bump. Nervous energy? She knew the feeling!

"Just got home from work," he said, smoothing a palm across his bare abs. "It's, uh, almost midnight."

"What? Oh my gosh." That the client had found her sleeping in his closet! And it was so late! "I can't believe I slept so long. I should leave. We'll reschedule our initial assessment for tomorrow. I'm so sorry, Senor Vasquez. I—this is not like me at all. I'm much sharper. Totally reliable."

Futile attempts to keep her eyes from his abs were just that—futile. He didn't seem the least embarrassed.

"Don't worry about it. You're here for about a week?"

"Yes, a week. Or so. However long it takes to complete your compatibility assessment and... to get you matched."

"Assess all you like. I have confidence your AI will find my true love."

"Yes, true love." Delivered by artificial intelligence. Oh, how Amber despised AI. It had taken her job, after all. Yet despite that annoyance, she would only speak positively about its ability to delve into the realm of romance and love for the client. It was what the job required. "What everyone desires."

He cocked his head at her. "I don't have to

know you to judge from your tone that you just lied to me. Don't you believe in love, Amber?"

"Of course, I do." Mercy, she was so tired. Not top of her game. He'd easily sussed out her lie. "And you will too once the algorithms report back with your perfect match."

"I'm excited to begin the process. I called Lux Love because I don't have the time to do this on my own. And I'm over swiping left or right."

The norm for a man of his income level. As well, those who were financially gifted required a vetting service to weed out the gold diggers and transactional seekers. Unless of course, that was the sort of relationship the client sought.

"Please consider my home your home while you are here. I like to know my guests are treated as family."

"Gracias."

"You'll stay in the guest room while you are working?" he asked.

"Oh." Amber gestured toward the narrow window. "I have a room at a nearby hotel."

"Nonsense." A swipe of his fingers through his hair dispersed some hanks from his eyes. Dark irises that she couldn't get a good read on. But his smile distracted from that assessment. Genuine but a little nervous, to assess his fidgety movements. "There are so many guest rooms in my home even I don't know how many there are. I've had Maria prepare one for you. It'll be good to have you on-site, and you'll save some expenses."

"My boss would certainly appreciate that. And it is very late—"

"The guest room it is," he interrupted.

"But I've had my suitcase sent to the hotel."

He tapped his watch and spoke into it in Spanish, which Amber was able to half-decipher. "Maria, are you still awake? Come bring Senorita Martin to one of the guest rooms, will you? No, she's not Emmer, she's Amber. *Amber.* Like… the tree resin." He winked at her. A comment from Maria sparked him to correct her. "No, the orange trees don't need trimming. Come to my closet, Maria."

Amber looked to the door, possibly for escape. She'd just experienced the absolute worst possible way to meet the client. Colette must never learn about this less-than-promising beginning.

"My housekeeper will be right up."

"I hope you didn't wake her. I can find the room on my own."

"No worries. She stays up late watching her stories. Let her know which hotel your suitcase is at. I'll have my car pick it up for you." He scratched the back of his head. Could he have a manner that did *not* draw her gaze to those killer abs? "There's some grass in the courtyard. You can access it from any of the guest rooms."

"Uh, grass?"

Valentino's smile was sweet but salted with a curl of sensuality. "Take off your shoes and ground yourself. It's good for jet lag. It's what I do after a long flight. Works like a charm. So we can begin tomorrow?"

"Of course. I'll want to tour your home, take things in." *Assume control.* "Everything I observe will be entered in our database to complete your profile."

"Usually I wake at five for a jog, then head in to work after the sun has risen."

"Oh."

He smirked. "You've got free rein of the house. Do what you need to do. I'll check in with you at a more fitting hour to see if you have questions?"

She nodded. "That sounds great. I appreciate your hospitality, Senor Vasquez."

"It's gotta be Val if you're going to move in for a few days."

"Val. Of course."

"And you are Amber."

"Tree resin," she said and then burst into a big sleep-deprived grin.

He winked at her just as Maria called down the hall. "She'll get you set up. Don't forget to ground!"

* * *

Val watched the woman in a sleek red suit with sleep-mussed hair—he hadn't pointed that out to her—walk out, noting she clung to her purse as if it were a shield. Her legs went on for days. And despite her slim hips, she had the sexiest wiggle to her backside. She was going to spend a week with him to ensure he found the perfect match?

Something he didn't have the time, or social IQ, to do on his own. All the apps he'd given a try never showed the real person. Everyone lied about something. But the Lux Love service was something he could get behind. They utilized proprietary algorithms to find a match. As a gaming coder, he trusted algorithms.

He'd been told the Lux Love lifestyle consultant would assess his home, workplace, his every move. As a consultant, she may even suggest tweaks or slight lifestyle changes that may enhance his dateability. She would even go out on dates with him to assess how he treated a woman. That was all fine with him.

It wasn't going to happen naturally. So when all else failed, AI had his back.

With one last glance to catch the towel-clad backside of the finest Spanish billionaire she had ever met—admittedly, the only one—Amber followed the housekeeper's rapid steps. Maria curled down the grand staircase and they crossed the inner courtyard. Another bubbling fountain? More tiles? Terra-cotta planters? Love it! The home's decor held immense visual appeal for Senor Vasquez's future match.

But Amber knew that was all surface. The true measure of a perfect match lay in understanding her client's emotional wants and needs. Body language was an excellent indicator of emotion. Valentino's body language had been easy and sensual yet a little anxious. Of course, their meeting had been out of the ordinary.

They continued around a corner on the ground floor and down a hallway, then Maria opened a door, flicked on the inner light and gestured for Amber to enter. The spacious room drew her inward. Bright curtains were pulled back to reveal the solar lights set here and there in the courtyard.

Grounding? Was the man into that woo-woo stuff? She wouldn't expect that from a tech genius.

"Is good," the housekeeper stated. Not as a question.

"Yes, it's—yikes!" Amber jumped back after almost stepping into the large taxidermy head of a bull. Stuffed and mounted on a massive wood plaque. The horns were tipped in gold. It sported a large ring through its nose. "What the… Uh, is this…?"

She turned but Maria was gone.

Shaking her head at the dispassionate maid, Amber stepped wide around the hideous thing. It had been set on the floor in the corner of the room; the big black glossy eyes focused directly on the bed.

Hands to her hips, she took a step back and wondered if she could ask for a different room, then thought better of it. She was a solutions person. This? A challenge to be met.

She spied a blanket spread across the end of the bed. With a grand swing, she managed to cover the bull's horns and… Those eyes still held her in uncertain panic.

"You are going elsewhere," she said with a waggle of her forefinger at the beast. "And then, to tackle the rest of this place. And…"

The man had stood before a complete stranger in nothing but a towel. Valentino Vasquez certainly wasn't modest. Had he been goading her? Looking for a reaction? Some men were so full of themselves they thought the entire female population wanted them. She hadn't sensed that from Valentino. Val. And she wouldn't lodge a single complaint against studying his body.

On the other hand, she was not here to assess

his physique. Beyond checking the box that he appeared healthy.

"A fine specimen," she whispered. The sudden wave of heat that rosed her neck and cheeks could not be a blush.

Amber Martin was *not* attracted to Valentino Vasquez.

Colette's voice echoed in her head: *Don't fall in love.*

"And don't forget it."

Because love was fickle and never lasted. And after trying to console her dad during her recent visit, who still had not gotten over her mother, heartbreak was not something Amber wanted to experience.

CHAPTER THREE

AMBER SLEPT WELL despite the watchful eye of the bull. Today she would go through Val's house to get a feel for his environment. Most would believe it wasn't necessary to go so deep into a person's life just to make a match. Did the match really care if his sheets were flannel or silk? If his toothpaste was all-natural? And were those tiles in the courtyard mass-produced or handmade here in Seville? It was Lux Love's dedication to detail that had garnered them a 98 percent success rate.

Amber's boss never talked about that 2 percent. She did wonder about it but would never ask. Inappropriate. And…they couldn't get it right all the time, could they?

Well. She did expect that a computer should make that a 100 percent with ease.

Now she stood out in the courtyard barefoot on the grass surrounding the orange trees. Having discovered a plate of fresh fruit, coffee and toast waiting for her in the kitchen, along with a text from Val: Left for a jog at five a.m. Feel free to go through the house while I'm at work. As well, he'd given her the code to his closet. Just in case, he'd noted and ended with a smiley face emoji.

She would not carry that humility of getting trapped in his closet. It had happened. She had not seen *all* his anatomy. Unfortunately. Nothing she could do now to change that inauspicious first meeting. Move on.

But as well, check the box for *thoughtful* and *kind.*

Wiggling her toes in the cool grass, she gave herself a gold star for insinuating herself into the client's home. Colette preferred on-site vetting, but her consultants booked hotel rooms first. If offered, they gracefully accepted to stay in the client's home, or guest house. And with the Lux Love clientele's income, that was generally offered.

Valentino Vasquez should be an easy match. Who could resist that muscular, dark drink of sexy? His voice oozed a playful sensuality. Amber shivered to think of it. Or was it the play of the grass across her bare toes that gave her the chill? No, the right tone of voice always did it for her. And his dark hair and beard stubble. Perfect playground for someone's fingernails to glide over. Explore. Dash a finger across his lips?

Straightening and shaking her head, she admonished herself for a slip into daydreams. She was not here to drool over the client. Swooning over a man was beneath her. She would note all the man's physical pluses on her assessment. And really? A person's exterior was just for show. What really mattered were the insides, and that included all the messy emotional stuff that, admittedly, she wasn't tops in relating to.

Stepping back into her heels, she gave her bouncy curls a flip with her hand then strolled inside. Her suitcase had been waiting outside her bedroom door this morning. Thankfully, she'd packed a linen dress for her visit to her dad, because it had been an unseasonable sixty degrees in Minnesota—crazy for the end of March. She visited her dad twice a year to catch up, but also to have coffee with friends from her hometown. Eddie Martin was an electrician who kept himself busy with work and outdoor sports like fishing and hockey with his friends. But he had been heartbroken when her mom announced she wanted a divorce three years ago. The pain in his eyes was still evident. Amber suspected her dad would never remarry. But she did hope he'd find a way toward seeking female companionship. There was nothing wrong with beers with the guys, but he had mentioned how he missed going to the movies and having dinner out.

Mom lived in Canada; she and Amber hadn't

seen one another in years. They were both still cooling off after what Amber considered a mutiny from what she'd thought had been a fairy-tale romance of twenty-five married years. The luster had been wiped from her mom's veneer. She'd not been the perfect wife, after all. The divorce had crushed Amber's heart and made her believe that love could never be real. If two people could part after living together so long? Why risk even entering into a relationship in the first place?

But right now, in order to do her best at the matchmaking gig, Amber had to set that heartbreak aside.

The entire Vasquez villa smelled like an orange tree orchard. It was going to be quite a letdown to return to her tiny space in Paris that backed up to a brick wall. But still. Paris. A girl could never argue with that cosmopolitan address. Even if it was merely a closet. And paying rent put her in debt.

She picked up the Lux Love–issued tablet she'd left in the kitchen and decided to go through the house room by room. It was surprising what could be learned about a person by taking in their surroundings. Artwork was a big personality tell. While furniture and the colors and textures within the house were considered, many men of Val's wealth used stylists, minimizing its importance. She would even spy on his television watch list. All sports and no movies? Only documentaries? Romances and action-adventure? All necessary to get a thorough understanding of the client.

First confirming the housekeeper wasn't around, she then opened some kitchen cupboards to get a feel for what foods Valentino Vasquez liked to eat. Hmm, there were a lot of orange preserves in here.

Val stepped out of the lounge chair he'd designed to optimize his working conditions. A comfy chair, it sported a full-body massager, heat and cold adjustments, and was equipped for VR with haptic sensors. When not sitting, he stood on the hologram platform amidst a literal digital representation of his work. Thanks to the room's biosensors, he could type and move code around without haptic gloves. It was action-movie futuristic stuff, but not really. This was today's technology, and he loved playing with it. But there was also an hourly alarm to alert him to give his brain a rest. Otherwise, he could get lost here in "the dark room," and may emerge in the middle of the night. Been there. Done that far too many times.

His brain worked best when immersed in chaos. He rarely grounded himself like he'd told Amber to do last night. But he should. He wasn't going to find a life partner by spending 75 percent of his time here in the dark room. Or was it eighty? He didn't want to do that math.

A glance to his watch confirmed it was lunch time. The cafeteria catered from local restaurants and always offered something delicious. As he left the room, he said goodbye to Hal, the AI he'd programmed to help him code and which biomonitored the entire dark room. Hal could tell him he was going to get a cold before Val even knew it. Everything about the Verdadero headquarters was designed for health. Both he and Teo were sticklers for working out, staying healthy and…

Teo had fallen in love last year. He'd found his person. And had married her recently. And that had poked at Val's heart in a manner he hadn't expected. Made him examine his life. What little life he had away from the office. He wanted that happy, smiling, confidant stride Teo had. And after years of devoting all his time and talent toward Verdadero, he wanted to start focusing on his needs. Was it possible? What *were* his needs?

The main need had risen to the fore after missing his regular weekly dinner engagement with his dad last week. Luis Vasquez had wanted to introduce his son to a niece of a family friend. His old man was always trying to get him married off. To start a family. To preserve a family legacy steeped in cultural traditions. And Val didn't mind; it distracted his dad from bemoaning his son's job.

You have so much talent! Luis Vasquez often accused his son. *What is this coding? It is not a traditional skill.* And then his dad would make that scoffing noise and the gesture of dismissal the old man should patent. Luis had actually once told a news reporter that his son had been lured away from dancing by the selfish pursuit for money. Seriously!

His dad was a former bullfighter. Luis once lived for the adulation, the cheers from the crowd. He'd married a beautiful Andalusian flamenco dancer for love. Since Val could walk, his mother had influenced him to take up flamenco dance. He loved the movement, the expression of a story that was steeped in Andalusian and Sevillian history.

There were times Val wondered if he'd made the right choice leaving dance for coding. It hadn't been for money; but, oh, how the money had flowed. He did enjoy his job *and* he worked with his best friend. Who could ask for anything more?

He could. He wanted love. And to start his own family. And sure, he could assuage the guilt his dad instilled by marrying a Spanish woman.

But he'd missed the dinner date. Why could he never remember to schedule appointments in his calendar? Luis had called and chewed him out. Val had given the usual excuse: working. So when Teo had sent him a link to Lux Love a few days later, Val had immediately called the number and spoken to the owner, Colette Bellerose. He was ready to get serious about finding love.

But what a tease that they'd sent a gorgeous woman to live with him for days to vet him for the service. And to find her sleeping in his closet? That seemed far off course from a professional dating service, but he did understand she had been jet-lagged and had appeared embarrassed. He'd decided against trying to speak to her this morning. His hours were too early for most humans.

She would go on dates with him to see how he treated a woman? Fair enough. But also, not fair! How to keep from staring at her bright red lips? From pushing his fingers through that bouncy dark hair? Sleep tousled, it had been so…touchable. But he'd read that clutched purse as uptight. That would have to change. No one spent any amount of time with him without letting down their hair and eventually going for a jog with him.

It was his nature. He was *inquieto*, as his mom used to describe his need to always move, always be doing something—creating, running, dancing, coding, whatever was to hand. He couldn't sit still for long. Even when coding, he paced the holo-platform, gesturing, jogging, shadowboxing. He kept a jump rope in the dark room for quick bursts of adrenaline. And his brain insisted on remaining in the game, short-circuiting his focus and constantly alerting him to new tasks, experiences, tastes, conversations—whew!

He tired himself out some days.

"Val!"

At the sound of his partner's voice, Val jumped into a spin and waited for Teo to catch up with his backward steps. "Heading in for some gazpacho. Join me?"

"Always." His friend since middle school was taller than him, a good-looking guy and very driven. Teo was somber to Val's goofy. And always dressed impeccably.

Val had tried to do business suits but his constantly-in-motion body struggled with the strict confines, so he went with jeans and a T-shirt most days. But a nice T-shirt. So what if it had a few wrinkles?

Teo opened the glass cafeteria door and held it as Val dashed inside. "How's the StarCloud project coming along?"

"With all our games now being considered as potential movie projects, I want to go over everything with a fine-tooth comb." They'd signed a deal with a major movie studio last year to put *Matador* on the big screen. Their former partner, Pablo, who had died years earlier, would be so proud! "How about you? What are you working on?"

"This and that. Marketing the latest VR gaming centers we opened last month in Japan. You remember there's the foundation ball in less than two weeks, right?"

The men sat at their usual table and with a gesture to the chef from Teo, they knew they'd be served.

Val leaned back and put his foot up on an empty chair. His favorite trainers were getting thin on the rubber soles. They were about the only material item he enjoyed shopping for. "I forgot about the ball."

"I knew you would." That smile was the one Teo always gave Val when he knew his friend's brain was juggling half a dozen balls.

Val nodded thanks to the chef, who delivered their meals personally. "What's the focus for this one?"

Every year Verdadero held an elegant ball to thank the supporters of the Pablo Pascal Foundation. One third of Verdadero's profits, Pablo's share, was placed in the foundation. It was their way of giving back to the community they loved and to honor their departed friend Pablo, who had been killed in a tragic hit-and-run crash; the driver had had a medical emergency. Twenty-two had been too young to die. But Pablo's legacy would live forever through the foundation and in their original game, *Matador*.

"Your suggestion, actually," Teo said. "Remember the meeting after the last ball when you said we should donate to local schools to pay for music education and instruments?"

"Oh yeah, that was my idea. Cool. It's time to dig out my tux."

"And consider having the shirt ironed, eh?"

Val matched Teo's smirk. Maria—she tried to keep up with him but laundry was not her forte. Nor was housecleaning. But she could mix up a to-die-for sangria.

"Cara is excited for the event. It'll be her first one as my wife."

She and Teo had married recently after dating a year. Cara had once dated Pablo. After the car accident and following Pablo's funeral, she had disappeared. Then last year she'd shown up in a Sevillian hospital in need of a place to stay while she recovered from surgery to remove her burst appendix. Teo had taken her in. And that was another story entirely.

Val high-fived his best friend across the table. "She's good for you."

"Too good for me," Teo said. "She makes sure I don't get bogged down in work and that I laugh at least once a day. But am I good enough for her?"

"Never." Val chuckled. "But I won't tell her that."

"Do keep that to yourself. So what about you?

Did you look into that matchmaking service I suggested for you?"

"There's a consultant at my home right now, going through it with a fine-tooth comb."

Teo slurped in some of the chilled soup. "What's that about?"

"They pour over my entire life in order to match me to the perfect woman."

"Do you *really* want a perfect woman?"

"Absolutely not. Perfect would be too much. You know what I really want?"

"A gaming partner who won't complain about your dirty boxers strewn all over the house?"

"Is someone like that available?"

They both laughed.

"No, what I really want is goose bumps love."

Teo nodded, knowing. They'd both listened to Pablo when they were teens talking about all the women he was going to love. Pablo had been geeky Val's inspiration and a mentor on how to approach girls. According to Pablo, the only way to know if you were really in love? A guy got goose bumps when he kissed the one.

It hadn't happened yet. But that was the measure Val intended to use.

Perfection was always her goal.

Amber had strived for it her entire life. From getting straight A's in school—the rewards were cash from her parents and a new laptop—to wearing trending clothes, even if she had to budget and find dupes or thrift, makeup and hair. She had to do things right. The perfect way. Or it wasn't worth doing at all. And so what if others didn't understand her quest for perfection? All that mattered was that metaphorical gold star she got when she knew the job had been done right. More so now that she was competing against her parents' failed marriage. They had lost their gold star. Amber was determined to keep hers.

Her shoulders dropped as she stood in the guest bedroom staring at the massive stuffed bull's head. There was a fine line she tried to balance between overzealous control and a breathable state of not-quite-control, yet it wasn't that easy. Perfection had been brewed into her veins by her professor mom and electrician dad. She didn't know how to let her hair down and relax. And that taxidermy head was not conducive to relaxation.

Her phone rang.

"Colette, how are you?"

"Amber, *chère*, you are in Seville with the client." Colette wasn't one for niceties; she always got right to the point. Unless you met her in person, then the double-cheek kisses and surface-level praise were de rigueur. "How was the initial meeting?"

In the closet and with a half-naked man? She couldn't tell her boss she'd fallen asleep on the job before the job had even started. The bull's glossy stare seemed to accuse her of that slipup.

She turned her back to the beast.

"Senor Vasquez keeps odd hours, so he was home late last night and out the door before the sun rose this morning. He's given me free rein in his villa and I've spent the day assessing the place."

"Any issues?"

"Other than a severe lack of tidiness, nothing stands out. The expected expensive artwork and furnishings. Electronic gadgets and toys everywhere." A superior coffee maker that she had merely told what she'd wanted and it had delivered. "Also very cozy and traditional. I like it." She straightened, realizing she'd interjected her own feelings. "I mean, it's a lovely home. But I may suggest he hire a housekeeper."

"I thought he already had one. His survey lists a chef, gardener and maid."

Yes, Maria. Amber wasn't sure what the woman actually did around the house. She'd only seen her in the kitchen at lunchtime, sitting at the table watching a portable television. She'd barely lifted her head to tell her to help herself to the pantry items. Or at least, that's how she'd interpreted her rapid Spanish.

"It's the first day," Amber stated, unwilling to

let on that she hadn't gotten a grasp on the job yet. "I'm just sitting down to fill in data on the assessment."

"Have you scheduled a date with Senor Vasquez? We mustn't waste time, Amber. We don't want to impose on the client longer than necessary. Efficiency is key."

"I'm very efficient." And she expected the validation for that. But she hadn't looked ahead to the date part of this assessment. And that wasn't because this was her first time in the field. She was…a little nervous? Unsure about doing the fake date thing with such an arrestingly handsome man? "I'll…we'll go out tonight so I can get a feel for how he treats a woman."

"Excellent. Keep us updated. I'll be following your progress as the data comes in."

"Of course."

"Ciao."

"Yes, ciao," Amber muttered but Colette had already hung up.

Her boss was a stickler for keeping the budget down, but she also strived to keep an elite face to the company. Which required her consultants to dress the part, checkbook groaning. Necessary, considering their clientele. Invited to all the hottest parties, Colette often mingled with the rich, celebrities and even politicians. But behind the scenes she was all business and aiming to move that 98 percent match rate up another number.

Amber dialed Val and when he didn't answer, she texted: Would you like to get something to eat tonight? Work date?

He answered quickly. You going to study me?

Of course.

Sounds intriguing. I'll be home early, around seven.

See you then, she texted back.

She wandered to the patio door and stepped out, taking off her shoes. Her skin tingled, soaking in the citrusy scent. Muscles shivered from a cool breeze. She was going on a date with a man she'd met briefly last night. In a towel. And she'd taken that time to count his abs—an eight-pack—instead of holding a witty, informative conversation with him.

Who would have ever thought a girl who had once aspired to sit in dusty old law libraries researching for her bosses would see herself in such a situation? It hadn't been in her life trajectory. So did that mean she was adaptable?

"Don't get carried away," she muttered. "The last thing you want to do is let your hair down and…" *Have fun?* "…screw up this job."

CHAPTER FOUR

EXITING THE SHOWER after work, Val wandered into his bedroom with a towel wrapped about his hips. He rubbed another towel over his wet hair. Arriving home around 10:00 p.m., he'd found Amber sitting at the kitchen table rapping her fingers on the surface. That look she'd given him had felt like a parent admonishing a child. Had she studied under Luis? Ha! So he'd been three hours late. Yes, he knew he couldn't do that on a *real* date.

If he were honest with himself, it wasn't because he couldn't remember to schedule appointments or to leave work at a reasonable hour—it was just that his priorities were focused on work. He didn't know how to move *personal life* up on that list.

Kind of weird to think that Senorita Martin was meticulously scrutinizing his life, both personally and professionally, to find him the ideal partner.

The one woman for him. His person.

Was she out there?

Changing into casual slacks and a black dress shirt, he then studied his face in the vanity mirror. Needed a shave, but he'd not known his face without the dark stubble since he was a teenager. Giving his hair a vigorous scrub with his hands would help it to dry. He kept it trimmed along the sides and back and let the top do its thing. A woman had once told him in a sultry coo that it was bed-tousled. Ha! The sight of his messy morning hair would have made her laugh.

On his way to the main level to find Amber, he passed Maria resting in the inner courtyard under an orange tree. The mini TV was propped before her.

"How's the family, Maria?" he called as he strolled down the stairs.

"Eduardo and Catalina are having an affair."

"No kidding?" He jumped from the second to the bottom step to the tiled floor. "That's not good."

"Oh, it's delicious."

He smiled to himself at his housekeeper's giggle. Over the years, he'd gotten to know all the names of the soap opera characters that kept Maria's attention. "I'm heading out, Maria. Don't wait up for me."

He always said that to her when he left. She wasn't his mother, or even his grandmother, but she was a sort of matriarchal substitute. His mother had passed away when he was seventeen. He'd not known grief until then; he'd felt her absence as a genuine ache in his heart. He was thankful for Teo and Pablo—they'd helped him to rise above that grief. Yet as he'd entered university, he struggled with leaving dance behind. The one thing that had bonded him and his mother. It had been Maria, who had worked in a local café near the campus, who had taken him under her wing, chatting to him as he'd burned late hours studying in the back booth. When he'd bought this villa, he'd gone in search of Maria and learned she was doing housekeeping. Good woman, that Maria.

Amber spun out of the kitchen in a knee-length blue dress that more than hugged her body. It wrapped its metaphorical arms about her and made love to her. She wasn't a curvaceous woman, but something about the way she held herself, chin up, shoulders straight, radiated confidence. Her hair was so shiny. Val wanted to touch it, see if those curls might coil about his fingers. And how perfect was her mouth? The bright red lipstick screamed that her mouth had been made for a kiss.

"Senorita Martin." He bowed slightly. "Nice to finally meet you. Er…in the proper manner.

My apologies for last night. I hadn't expected to find you—"

"Awake and upright? Already forgotten," she rushed out. She extended her hand for him to shake. The greeting was too formal. He stepped in and kissed both her cheeks. She slipped back, a little startled. "I, uh… Nice to meet you too, Senor Vasquez. Despite the three-hour lag." She wasn't going to let him forget about his lateness. "And thank you for giving me the run of your home today while you were at work."

"Did you find what you were looking for?"

She tilted her head in question. "I wasn't snooping, or anything like that. I noted how you live. If there are possible areas for improvement—"

"Improvement? You don't like my casa?"

"It's lovely. The artwork tells a lot about a man."

"You think so?" Val turned to the Dulk mural on the wall behind him. "How do you know that wasn't there when I moved in?"

"Generally, when someone with your kind of money moves into a house, they usually make it their own. Including the artwork. I can't imagine you'd be content with another person's tastes."

"Unless they match my own?" He shook his head. "I'm teasing you. That's my favorite work." He gestured over his shoulder. "Dulk is an urban artist. He worked directly on the wall with spray paints and oils. The fish on the leash always gives me a chuckle. You like the modern artists?"

"I'm not into art all that much. I wouldn't know a Picasso from a Rembrandt."

"Oh, you would. But now don't think I'm going to forget you mentioned something about improvements? To my home?"

"I shouldn't have put it that way. Well. I'm looking at your home as if I were a potential match. Women like a tidy home. Everything in its place. How else to know what belongs and what doesn't?"

Val smirked. "That's what a cleaner is for."

"That's what I've always understood, but…"

That she let it hang was a play, inviting his move. So Maria did not pull her weight around here. It didn't bother him at all.

Val snagged a pair of black loafers from beneath a stack of unread newspapers that were creeping out from the foyer closet and slipped them on. "Maria is non-negotiable. She stays. No matter what."

"Is she…family?"

"Yes. Uh…not by blood, but she's been with me since I got this place six years ago."

Amber made an adjustment to his shirt collar. Comfortable with him already? Or some kind of neat freak? He guessed the latter. Everything about her was exact and tidy.

She splayed her fingers and stepped back, obviously realizing her faux pas. That moment of self-realization tickled him. Like she wanted to relax and go with the flow but had to stop herself. He'd not known such a restrained person as she. Interesting.

"I shouldn't have presumed," she said. "Whatever help Maria provides is certainly worth it if she's like family to you. But an occasional stop-in from a cleaner..."

"I can look into that. I'll add it to my list of things to do." Which needed to move up on his priority list. Hell, what priority list?

She smelled like the orange blossoms with a hint of warm spice. The urge to wrap an arm around her waist and pull her closer was so strong he had to inwardly admonish the lusty thought. No flirting with the consultant! "Too many wrinkles?"

"Just the one right here." She pressed her fingers over his shoulder. "If I buy you an iron..."

"I do know that I own an iron. One talent Maria has is she puts a nice crease in my boxers. You gotta love that."

"Well then." She stepped back, hands to her hips in assessment of her handiwork. "Creased boxers. I'll add that to your profile."

"Really?"

She shook her head. "No."

"Ah, so you've some funny in you." He hooked an arm and she threaded hers with his. "I'm completely in your hands tonight. *Matchmaker, matchmaker, make me a match*," he sang as he opened the front door and led her through the courtyard to meet the waiting car.

"*Catch me a catch*," she sang in response. "I love *Fiddler on the Roof*."

"Yeah? I like the old musicals, too. Great way to divert my brain from code during an afternoon break." He opened the car door for her. "Your carriage, my lady."

"Why thank you, good sir."

Once inside, he noticed Amber's dismay at the instrument-free dashboard.

"It's driverless," he said. "The AI does it all."

"Oh. AI. Of course. Yet one more thing set on taking over the world."

Val smirked. "And I'm happy about it. Buckle up. We'll be there in no time."

Sitting in a car that drove itself was unnerving. Val hadn't once touched the steering wheel. In fact, he'd slid his seat back and leaned an arm on the side door. Amber twisted her fingers under her thighs as he pointed out sights along the way.

Oblivious to the worry they could crash at any moment.

Get over your annoyance at AI, Amber. It wasn't so much that she hated it. If the car were suddenly presented with an accident situation, would it choose to swerve to avoid a pedestrian, thus saving its occupants, or go straight ahead, possibly killing an innocent?

Oh, she had to stop thinking about it. *Concentrate on the sexy man. Take notes for his future wife. Do your job.*

Soon enough they'd arrived, Amber grabbed the door handle, eager to get out of the bizarre car, but then she relented. Would he run around and open the door for her?

When her door opened, and Val offered his hand, she took it, mentally noting that this one was a gentleman.

CHAPTER FIVE

ONCE AT THE RESTAURANT, Val got out of the car and swung around the back to open Amber's door and help her out. When she started to walk, he hooked his arm in hers and strolled her through the front door. The gentlemanly moves startled her. Amber hadn't been privy to such an act of chivalry. Ever. This was definitely going to make his score soar.

The restaurant was cozy but classy. At sight of Val, the maître d' escorted them to a table on a private terrace set near a fragrant flowering vine. Though the temperature had fallen, a nearby open hearth kept the area warm. Candlelight glittered. Somewhere, a soft melody was sung by a live singer. The waiter filled their wineglasses. Amber already felt more special than any date she'd previously—

She had to check herself. *She* was not on a real, romance-possible date with Val. This was a business date so she could get a feel for how the client treated a woman. And it hadn't started out on the best foot. She'd waited for him for hours.

Upon sitting, she'd set the tablet to her left, opened to the notes page.

"Does that tablet come along for the ride all the time?"

"I am on the clock." Amber sipped the crisp wine. "There're thousands of data points to complete your profile. I'm not much of a techie, but I know our proprietary AI is the key to Lux Love's success rate."

"Ninety-eight percent is nothing to sneeze at. Yes, the more data you enter, the finer and more accurate your results will be. But let's pretend this is a real date, *sì*? I haven't been on a date in a while and—honestly, it's a rarity I get to relax and talk to a beautiful woman."

The comment should make any woman glow but Amber couldn't recall ever blushing. Though the feeling of warm acceptance was awesome. Even if it was fake, she could enjoy the compliment. And, very well, she needed to relax a little in order to take in the full experience.

"Right. This should be like a real date." She tucked the tablet in her purse. "Sorry. I'll take notes later. I…just like things to be perfect."

"Perfection is unobtainable."

"I don't know." The way the candlelight glinting in his dark irises was surely some sort of romance addict's prompt to fall into them. Amber halted her fall by sitting up straighter. "Ahem. I'm sure I can touch perfection. It's on my life trajectory."

"Your life trajectory? What's that about?"

"This date is not about me."

"But it is." He leaned forward, propping his elbows on the table, totally at ease in his body. "I like to get to know a woman when I take her on a date. Not talk about myself."

A man interested in something other than his stunning bank statement and remarkable intellectual feats? Intriguing.

"Fine." She could play along. And really, providing personal anecdotes would make the client more open to sharing his personal details.

Amber teased the stem of her wine goblet to distract her interest from his gaze. She'd once watched a movie set in the Regency era where the heroine had described the hero's eyes as brooding. She hadn't understood what that meant. Until now. Val's dark, heavily lashed eyes were definitely broody. Like sex simmering, waiting for the right moment. To…what?

Oh, she just wasn't tops when it came to dating. Once upon a time, she'd believed in love. Looked forward to the man opening her car door and treating her like a queen. Since her parents' divorce had shattered that belief in love? Her idea of a date was to be set up by a friend, go out for drinks and if both were willing, a few hours of making out and sex. Always at his place. And she always left right after sex. She didn't do the snuggle. Too awkward.

But none of that personal stuff would be revealed to a client. Unnecessary.

"My life trajectory," she announced. "Pay off my bills. Paris is very expensive. Start my own business. I'm not sure it has to be matchmaking related. It has to play to my strengths."

"Your strength is *not* in matchmaking?"

Oops. Shouldn't have mentioned that one. "Well, of course." Amber fiddled with the goblet stem. "Or else I wouldn't be here right now. I'm skilled in reading body language." Two days of utilizing it so far! "Your relaxed position means you are open. Easygoing. But as for the rest of my trajectory—" Yes, distract from the sad truth that she wasn't the best person to know and recognize love. That's what the algorithms were for. "—I want to own a home. Either in a city or suburbs. I'm not picky. But I prefer international as opposed to the States. I'm loving Spain so far. This spring weather is great, but I've heard Seville is like a frying pan in the summertime."

"You have to know how to live. Rise before the sun, spend the sunny hours inside with the air-conditioning, and siesta in the afternoon. It's all good. But one thing I didn't hear in your trajectory was mention of romance."

"Romance?"

Watch it, Amber. That tone of disgust is not putting a good light on Lux Love.

"Isn't that what life is about? To love and be loved?"

Could the man be any more compelling? His eyes...lured. She couldn't look away from them. And then his whole face came into view and his easy body language held such a teasing appeal. He wasn't trying too hard. Wasn't spouting numbers and successes like most men were wont. He seemed genuinely interested in the topic.

"Love has its merits," she said by rote. "I suppose."

"Wait." Val laid a hand on the table, skimming her fingertips that rested on the base of her wine goblet. A practiced move? Subtle touching could clue to seeking control. "A consultant from a matchmaking service is telling me that love *has its merits*?" One of his fingers tapped one of hers. "Do you even believe in what you sell?"

"I didn't mean it that way." Not the way to sell the company. She could hear Colette firing her right now. "I just...well..." Exposing her private life wasn't necessary to matching this man to another woman, but... His finger tapped hers again. A little tease or a touch of assurance? Amber sighed. “Love is personal to me. I don’t share intimate details on a first date.”

“I’m trying to get to know you.”

“But only for fake. This isn’t real, Val.”

“I know that, but I’m trying to be myself and you are making that difficult.”

“I’m sorry. I…know.”

By all means she had to win the client’s trust. She was his first match after all. Client to consultant. And this was part of the job. Letting her hair down metaphorically and playing the role of a date.

“You’re right. You are only asking questions you would ask any woman on a date. Trying to get to know her. See if there’s something about her that sparks your interest.”

“Exactly.”

“Honestly?” Dare she confess? He seemed good-natured about all this. “I’ve been with Lux Love for a year. I’ve watched and learned. But you’re my first field assignment. So, please, don’t say anything to my boss about my slipups, most especially our first meeting. I was mortified.”

“To see me in a towel? I’m not sure how to take that.”

“That eight-pack you have is fabulous. I mean, that I noticed.”

That grin. Like a kid who’d just scored a whole bag of chocolate and didn’t have to share it. It was cute, and it suited his easy charm. Oh, how his dates were going to love him. "For future reference, I'll try to wear clothing every time we are together."

Way to spoil a girl's daydreams.

"Clothing is good for client-consultant interactions. But on a real date, I'm sure you can let that rule slide."

He tilted his head in surprise.

What had she said? Oh! Amber had never been so flustered by a man's presence. He was all around her. Comforting but also tinged with a seductive tease. "Sorry. I'm trying to be perfect—"

"Amber." Val took her hand. His touches had a duty. To relax her, to make her feel grounded and comfortable. Mission: Scrambled! "Let's set perfection aside for the night, *sì*?"

The man held her gaze longer than a few seconds, which breached a certain level of propriety and crooked a finger, luring her toward something more intimate.

"Amber?"

Beyond her thundering heartbeats she wrestled with her brain. *Be in the moment. Take it all in. Just pretend it's a date. A real one.* That was the only way she'd ever get a peek inside who Valentino Vasquez really was.

"Can we start over?" she asked.

Val released her hand and raised his wine goblet. “Hola, I’m Valentino Vasquez. Everyone calls me Val. *Encantado a de conocerle.*”

“Pleasure to meet you as well, Valentino. I’m Amber Martin. Er…well, you know, like tree resin.”

His laughter was hearty and deep from his chest. And Amber couldn’t even feel embarrassed by his reaction.

“You make me laugh, Amber. I like that.”

“Pretty sure I don’t have a humorous bone in my body.”

“Everybody has one or two. I’ll find them all.”

Oh, would he? And how exactly did he intend to do that? By word or by touch? The thought was so arresting, she was thankful when the waiter arrived tableside with their meals.

Val requested more wine, and then took her hand again. “Join me to say thanks for this meal?”

A religious man? Or simply thankful for the things he had. Nice. Amber nodded and silently said a *thank you.*

When Val dove into the food, he growled appreciatively. “This is so good. I love it when someone else cooks for me.”

“Isn’t that always?”

“You got me there. I appreciate that my bank statement allows me to afford a chef.”

“Do you want a wife to cook for you?”

He forked in a bite of his food. "If she wants to, that would be great. If not? There's the chef. I'd never want a woman to do anything just to please me."

"But some people's love language is acts of kindness toward others. So a woman may like to cook for you."

"I'm good with that. How do I know what *my* love language is?"

"I'll let you know once I figure it out." The assessment included a whole section on just that. "I think I could get used to a personal chef."

"Much better than all those potato omelets in college. Ugh."

"Is that where you met your partner, Mateo Ortiz?"

"We've been friends since secondary school after the councilor assigned me to tutor Teo and Pablo in maths."

"You all went to the same school?"

"Yes, we grew up in Triana. It's an older Sevillian barrio steeped in tradition. I was so thankful for that tutoring setup. Met the best friends of my life."

"And where is Pablo now? You listed him as a founding partner of Verdadero in your survey. But I noticed he's not mentioned as a fellow CEO?"

"Pablo passed away eleven years ago. He was

hit by a driver who suffered a medical emergency."

"Oh, I'm so sorry. I didn't realize. I should have known." Why had that important detail not shown on the survey? A background check should have uncovered that.

"I didn't include that information in the survey because it's not necessary to finding a wife. Although..." Val leaned back in his chair. "Pablo was the one to show me how to be comfortable around girls. And it was his artwork and idea for a storyline that we developed into our first VR game, *Matador*. He was so talented. Kindest man you'd ever want to know."

"You must really miss him."

"*Sì*. We honor him every year with a fancy ball in his name. The next one is in under two weeks. You'll have to attend."

"I'm not sure I'll be here that long. This process generally only takes a week or so."

He lifted his wine goblet for a toast. "Here's to making it last as long as that *or so* can be."

Charmed by his compelling manner, Amber clinked glasses with him. He wanted her to stick around for weeks? That would make this one very long assignment.

Yet, the thought of spending time with Val wasn't unpleasant. Sitting across the table from him, dining on fine food and wine did not feel at all like work. She could almost place herself in the position of some lucky woman who may become the man's future wife.

Actually, that would be helpful in her assessment. If she reacted to him on an emotional level, then any other woman should as well, yes?

Look at you, Amber, acing this assignment.

"Tell me about that mention of dance in your survey," she said. "Is it something you enjoy watching?"

"I studied flamenco dance for a long time."

He danced? Interesting. "Why did you decide to make the switch from dance to coding?"

"My friends and I had an idea for a video game that we were eager to create. I started coding for it while also dancing. After my mom died, I couldn't bring myself to dance anymore. I made the decision to set dancing aside right after entering college. My father will never forgive me for that choice."

"Oh?"

Val shrugged. "The old man is traditional. A *baille*, or male flamenco dancer, is the epitome of masculinity to him. He's a retired bullfighter. Ultra masculine. But also steeped in Spanish tradition, you know? It is a tremendous guilt I carry, trying to please him."

"Doesn't the fact that you've made a fortune turn his head just a little?"

"Not at all." Val cut into his steak. "He thinks I've sold out to some robotic future that is going to overtake humankind. Ha! Well, you never know, eh? Anyway, I've always been a geek. Never attracted the girls in school because I hadn't a clue how to speak that language."

"What language is that?"

"Love and romance, of course."

"But you said Pablo taught you how to be comfortable around girls?"

"Yes, he taught me the finer points to being 'a ladies' man.' Yet I still question myself every time I go on a date. I always think no one will get me."

Really? Even with all his money? Amber checked herself. She had come to understand that the Lux Love client list was different than most in that their money could attract all the wrong people. "That's why I'm here. To get you."

He laid his hand over hers. "Which is why I'm putting my trust in the matchmaking service. Algorithms, I trust."

Algorithms. All to do with an artificial intelligence. It had made her job with the law firm obsolete. And everywhere she had applied asked if she could work with AI. Going in, she hadn't known Lux Love relied so heavily on AI to match clients. The lack of personal touch offended her. But she wasn't going to quit. Paris! And from what she'd seen over the past year, the AI did seem to have a talent for matching people. But she was never going to start engaging with a chatbot. Abhorrent.

"How much do you work now?" she asked.

"Every day, except Sundays. All day. And, very well, some Sundays as well."

"What time to you get in to work?"

"It varies from six to ten in the morning. Then I sometimes don't return home until after dark. Well, you saw last night was late."

"And tonight was no early return either. That's a very long workday. Making a match is one thing, Val. It's *keeping* that match that requires effort. Honing a relationship, and…working less, as you've already realized."

"My partner, Teo, is always telling me to work less. I don't even need to code. We've got many talented coders. And AI does a lot of the heavy lifting. But I can't seem to let go of it. I need to check their work. Make sure it's up to my standards."

"And is it?"

"Always."

"Then perhaps you need to accept that the job is being done well and that if you don't always have the opportunity to check their work, it'll be fine." Yet she could relate. Amber always checked her work over and over. No gold star for less than perfect! “Do you think I could tag along to your office tomorrow?” she asked. “Get a feel for your work life?”

“I’d love to show you around Verdadero. You want to tag along on the five a.m. jog too?”

Amber winced over a sip of wine.

“Had to try. I’ll return home around six to pick you up.”

She was an 8:00 a.m. riser. But this was her job, and she would do it to perfection.

“Six it is. Do you jog every morning?”

“Even in the rain, which is rare around here. Gets the blood rushing through my brain. I come up with the best ideas then.”

The waiter arrived with dessert. Val shrugged. “What’s a meal without a decadent dessert?”

Chocolate and cherry sauce? Oh, she was liking this man more and more.

Val suggested a walk along the river, which wasn’t far from his villa. They strolled on a sidewalk canopied by the city’s abundant orange trees.

“Your profile is filling in nicely,” Amber said. “But we need info on what you want in a woman. Looks, personality, education, career, values. All that stuff. You willing to go through the list?” She tugged her tablet from her purse.

Val shoved his hands in his pockets as they walked. “Fire away.”

“Okay, let’s start easy. Looks.”

“No, no. I’m not going to give you a description of what attracts me because I don’t know until I know.”

“Oh, come on. You don’t favor blondes over redheads? Slender over muscular? Petite over tall?”

“Never think about it too much. I like all sorts of women. I don’t judge a book by its cover, height or weight. Though, I suppose I should have checked *Spanish national* if I want to please my father. Which I do. And yet… I do adore dark brown curls.”

His wink startled her. *She* had dark brown curls.

“Don’t overthink that one. Next question,” he said.

“Fine. Open to all appearances with a preference for Spanish.” She made a note in her file. Hard not to feel self-conscious over her hair now. She pushed a hank of it over her shoulder. “How about occupations? Do you prefer a career woman? You seem to be looking for someone more traditional, so perhaps you prefer a woman who cooks and cleans and kisses you on the cheek every morning before you head off to work?”

"Is that an option? The cheek-kissing part? That would be cool."

"You're cute, but I'm trying to do my job. Cheek kisses are on the table," she said as she noted that. "What about her job?"

Val shrugged. "I am traditional in that I believe a woman shouldn't have to work to help support her family. I make more than enough money to cover a household so…a job isn't necessary. But."

She lifted a brow.

"If she enjoys working, I'm not going to tell her to stop. People take satisfaction in working. Especially work that plays to their passion."

"Passion is important," Amber said, because it sounded like the right thing to say. She wasn't sure if she had a passion. Even this job had been merely a means to move to Paris. It hadn't been because she'd been interested in matching people. Becoming a romantic fairy godmother, of sorts.

Yet, was that her future with Lux Love? For some reason, juxtaposing the algorithms with actual feelings and emotions never sat well with her. Was there a way she could bridge that gap and make things more personal for her clients?

What were they talking about? Passion. What would real, romantic passion feel like? And could AI ever find that for another person?

"Still taking notes?" Val's voice jarred her from her mind wandering.

"Uh, sure." She tucked away the tablet in her purse and inhaled. "It smells so good here under the orange trees. As does your house. You must miss it when the blossoms have dropped and lost their scent."

"A woman I once dated had an essential oil cologne crafted for me using *azahar*, the orange blossoms. I use it occasionally."

"What a lovely gift."

"*Sì*, I didn't know how to return the favor so I bought her a Vespa."

Amber's jaw dropped open.

"I know, right?" Val shrugged. "Our family has never been big on gifts. I don't know how to do them. They take a lot of thought. Do you think I should do gifts? For my dates?"

Being asked for guidance made her stand up straighter and a warmth curled in her chest. "Women do like gifts, but we don't need diamonds. Or Vespas. Simple things to show you notice are nice."

"I can do that." He leaped, tapping the canopy of leaves above them and landed before her. "Here." He twirled a big white blossom. "Just a little gift. Can I put this in your hair?"

"Uh…"

He stood close enough to inhale and oh, what a delicious man. Whose every spoken word and action made her realize how miserable her dating life had actually been up to this point. Lack of attentive lovers? Check. Never being able to maintain a relationship beyond a week or two? Unfortunate check. Passion? Not a single check. Allowing a man to touch her so casually without flinching? There was a first time for everything.

"Beautiful." Val's eyes dropped to her mouth. He lingered there, studying her as if she were the dessert they'd shared at the restaurant.

Panic curled at the base of Amber's throat. This felt very much like a go-in-for-the-kiss moment. Completely unacceptable for a Lux Love consultant to fraternize with the client. And yet…

What would his kiss feel like? To breathe him into her skin and taste his mouth… Hug against his strong frame and soak in his warmth like a starved kitten. It wasn't that she was against romance so much as she'd just never had a talent for it.

Suddenly, he stepped back. "Sorry. I, uh…" He rubbed his fingers along his jaw in an embarrassed move. "That was inappropriate. It felt like a kissing moment. *Sì*?"

Oh, yes, please yes! "A little."

"If this were a real date—"

"Oh, of course, I understand. Don't worry about it. I'm not offended." At not getting a kiss or that he'd thought she'd want one? What a liar, Amber!

"It's just that your lips are made for a kiss," he said in all seriousness.

"Oh my." Exhaling, her shoulders dropped. Her hair felt heavy on her shoulders, so…curly and dark. Like some kind of romance heroine. She'd never swooned over a man before. Had never stood in a moment like this. *Time to learn, Amber.*

"Whew!" Again, Val put some distance between them with a bouncy step and a bat at the low-hanging leaves. "Change the subject, man. I don't want to make you nervous." He bounced on his toes, shaking out his shoulders. Regrouping, in a manner. He gestured outward. "This is what I brought you here for. Check it out."

He led her through an aisle of trees to stand before a wrought iron balustrade that overlooked a drop to the river below. The dark blue velvet sky was sprinkled with stars. Breathtaking.

"I'm surprised you can see stars in the city," she said.

"You can always see the stars in Seville." He stood beside her, their elbows nudging. The heat of him overwhelmed her. The orange blossoms perfumed the air, giving her a woozy sort of contentedness. "This is why I will never leave Spain. It's so beautiful here."

"So you won't move for the woman you'll eventually fall in love with and marry?"

"It'll be a tough haul getting my feet off Sevillian soil."

"Noted."

"Stop taking notes, Amber. Just close your eyes and inhale. Then look to the glittering sky."

A romantic suggestion. She was going to make a note of that—later. Closing her eyes, she inhaled the *azahar.*

Had she just been thinking about swooning? Tossed her hair over a shoulder like…? Ha! And yet, he'd almost kissed her.

What was that about?

Best to focus on how securing this man his perfect match would get her a raise and pay those bills. It was all for her life trajectory. And his charming touches and gazes would never make her blush.

She was *impervious* to his charm.

"And don't forget it," she whispered to that wanting part of her that had surprisingly fluttered to life.

CHAPTER SIX

SHE WAS ADORABLE when sleeping. Val leaned over Amber's bed, hesitant to wake her. He'd already carefully pulled back the curtains from the window. If he were suave, he'd have swept her off her feet and into his arms already. Or at least, been more convincing last night. That stars-by-the-river moment had gone all wrong. He'd forgotten himself and had wanted to kiss her. That may work on a real date, but—this was like playing house and not getting the bonus of intimacy.

Could she feel the same? No, she was a trained professional. And he had contacted Lux Love for a reason. He trusted the algorithms. And in order for them to work, he had to play along with everything requested of him and provide all the data. So he could find the woman who would earn an approving nod from his dad. And that did not include being distracted by the sexy consultant.

Daylight was draining away. If the professional wanted to accompany him to work today to see that side of his life, it was time to get this show on the road.

"Sleeping Beauty!" he announced with the élan of a carnival barker.

Amber startled upright and caught her palms on the pillow. Hair tousled over her face, she looked around.

"Sorry," Val offered. It wasn't the kindest move. When was the last time he'd had a woman sleep over at his house and he *hadn't* slept with her? This situation was odd. But also kind of fun. "Had to be done."

Discombobulated, she slapped a palm toward the nightstand to grab her phone. "What time is it?"

"After seven."

"After—I set my alarm for six." She brought the phone closer to her face. "I hit snooze three times?"

"Sometimes the brain doesn't register those hits. It's that hypnopompic time of the morning where your memory plays tricks on you."

"Yes, that state of dreaming just before a person wakes. My apologies. I'm never late. I can't believe..."

Pushing the hair from her face, she looked at him. Her jaw dropped open. She clasped her arms across her chest. The blue-striped cotton pajama top and pants she wore didn't expose anything, but he sensed her sudden embarrassment.

Val turned and made to study the horns of the stuffed bull's head. "You know it is a great honor to receive such a gift from a matador?"

"Is that so? Did the bull win or lose? Either way—no. Don't tell me. I know it's a national tradition in Spain but if you ask me it's..." She gestured with a dismissive fling of her hand. "Do you always hover over sleeping women like that?"

"Not always. Sometimes I stare through their windows in the middle of the night." Her reaction was the expected shock. Val laughed and shook his head. "It's too early for my humor. Sorry. I'll leave you to get ready. Work is waiting."

"Yes, uh...give me half an hour."

"Is that all? I've never met a woman who can get ready in less than an hour."

Her eyebrow lifted in challenge. "Then make it twenty-five minutes."

"Deal." Val tapped his watch and set the timer as he strolled out of her room.

Amber made it in twenty-two minutes because that was how she rolled. Always up for a challenge. Shower, makeup, a tousle of her curly hair—no need to wash it. The linen sundress topped by a cashmere shrug was perfect for the weather.

The Spanish sun hit differently than in the States. It was golden and full and it felt as though her skin were sucking it in, starved of vitamin D following a long Parisian winter. And the air here wasn't like most big cities. It felt ancient, as if it possessed secrets never told, even through the centuries.

A bit of the fantastical slipping into her thoughts? Why not? Just because she was officially on the clock didn't mean she couldn't enjoy her surroundings. But she was thankful she'd missed the requisite jog. Val's car had driven them to his work, which was just across the river.

The Verdadero office occupied the top three floors in Torre Sevilla, the tallest office tower in Spain. Status symbol? Check. Val introduced Amber to Amaia, the receptionist who sported a pink bob, and who seemed to be handling three calls via her headset, pouring coffee to hand to Val and asking Amber if she took cream for hers. Amber loved her instantly.

"She's efficient," Val commented as they strolled through the halls that were a mix of grayish woods and steel. Masculine and modern. Spare in design. And lots of curved windows. Val peeked into his partner's office but Mateo Ortiz wasn't there.

"He's recently become a nine-to-fiver," Val commented as he gestured to another office across the hall. "That's mine, but I rarely use it. Too...office-like."

Sipping the coffee that tasted as if it had been freshly brewed from beans picked directly from the plant, Amber asked, "Isn't that what an office should be?"

"Sure, but stark walls and a desk are not me. I work in the dark room. It's my safe place."

That sounded both intriguing and a little worrisome. "What do you have to be kept safe from?" She followed his casual stroll up a stairway to the next floor.

"Interruptions." He cast a grin over his shoulder at her. "When I'm in the zone, I like to fly."

She knew his job involved sitting before a computer and typing mind-boggling lines of code that she couldn't begin to understand. And yet... "Doesn't AI do a lot of that nowadays?"

"It does, but someone's gotta tell the AI what to do. I do a lot of visual scripting and gesture-based coding, but good old-fashioned text-based coding is still the workhorse. In here."

Val opened a door that led into darkness and waited for her to enter. Amber paused on the threshold, clutching the coffee cup. This was the first time she'd felt the slightest bit of unease around him. He wasn't kidding about a dark room. "No lights?"

"When you step inside Hal will adjust to your presence."

"Hal?"

"The AI. A little *Space Odyssey* humor there. Go on. Hal won't bite. I don't think."

The man did try at humor. Amber had noted that in his assessment this morning after her rude awakening. Though, she had been the rude one missing their 6:00 a.m. wake-up call. And really, the joke could be very funny, but she had no context when it came to cyber stuff.

Stepping inside the cool room, it suddenly flickered and took on a greenish-white glow that made her feel as though she were standing inside a vast computer system. The entire far wall was a massive screen that scrolled code and looked like something from *The Matrix*. A huge easy chair sat before a black circular platform in the center of the room. The opposite wall featured a console with dozens of large monitors, keyboards and all the techie stuff she couldn't begin to name.

"This is where I work." Val slid a palm along the back of the leather chair. "My home away from home. And this is the captain's chair."

"It's certainly…" Cold. Busy. Unreal. Futuristic. "Exactly what I would expect for a man who codes for a living." But so opposite from the warm, charming man she was getting to know. "Quite fascinating. Why so dark?"

"The lighting is designed for optimal viewing and minimal eye strain. No blue light. Lots of healing yellow and red. It changes throughout the day and according to the inhabitant's biorhythms."

"The inhabitants? Even...me?" Amber scanned around for hidden cameras.

"Yes, you crossed a bioscanner upon entry. Hal is monitoring your every move."

"Creepy much?" She rubbed a palm up her arm, feeling the unease return. "And where was the informed consent?"

"Sorry. I don't often bring in visitors. I should have told you before entering. You can leave?"

"No, I'm fine. Not like we're not being recording everywhere we go and in every business we visit."

"You're not wrong."

Again, she scanned the walls and ceiling. "Is Hal recording everything we say?"

Val offered a sheepish shrug, which she took to mean *yes*.

With a gesture of his hand, the area above the circular pad suddenly filled with scrolling code. Very *Matrix*-like! Smiling, Val strolled to a wall where what looked like VR goggles were hung. Along with gloves and plastic swords and elaborate plastic guns. "Let me show you what I do. Have you ever experienced VR?"

"No." Amber reached out to touch the scrolling code and her hand moved through it. Fascinating. She had never gotten into video games. Not even *Words with Friends*, which was her dad's favorite time-waster. Save for her phone and a few social media accounts, she was as low-tech as it got. "But I'm interested in what you create."

"This is our latest prototype. Hope to bring it to market next year." Val held a silver visor toward her.

"It looks heavy."

"Nope. Made from ultralight carbon fiber. It's loaded with sensors, a gyroscope, accelerometer and cameras to track your movements. It's untethered so a person can move about freely. Are you…unsure?"

Beyond the need to learn more about what made the man tick so she could fill in his profile, the idea of standing beside him while they experienced altered worlds intrigued in a way that surprised her. Could she step into a fantasy world and be comfortable? Alone with this man who disturbed her personal boundaries with every slight touch he gave her?

"It doesn't hurt," he said encouragingly.

"I know that. I just…doesn't this mess with

your proprioception? I don't want to fall on my face."

By all means she would never put herself in a position to be appear unskilled or embarrassed.

"We've haptic feedback sensors to counteract issues with bodily placement. Come here."

He held out his hand and she took it. Because every time he touched her it made her feel things she'd never felt before. And she was curious about those feelings. It happened again as he led her into the platform so they stood amidst the code. Being led by this handsome being who seemed so gentle and whose touch made her skin scream *More!* Would his touch make any woman feel the same? He did like to touch, make skin contact. It was so natural to him he probably wasn't even aware.

Don't fall in love!

No. She wasn't that easy. And—when had he let go of her hand? She stared at her fingers for a moment. Lost.

"Do you get queasy easily?" he asked.

Queasy? From him holding her hand? It was more like a warmth in her belly that made her heart flutter. Her spine untense and—

Oh. No, he hadn't asked that. "Uh, no. I've a strong stomach."

The code moved over his face in flashes of

light. She wanted to touch the numbers on his face, but she kept her hands to herself.

"Good. The biometry system monitors your position and provides haptic feedback so it shouldn't make you dizzy, but some people are susceptible to inner ear fluctuations."

He displayed a glove which looked more like a chrome skeletal attachment one would wear on the back of their hand, with soft black sensors that curved over the fingers. "The bioglove is something new we're ready to put to market this fall. It allows you to touch and feel virtual objects. So you'll give it a try, *sì*?"

After she set the coffee cup aside, he showed her how to put on the gloves. They were incredibly lightweight. They did make her feel a bit like Skeletor. Then he helped her put on the visor.

With a wave of Val's hand, the scrolling code disappeared, leaving them in the subtle green glow of the room. "I'll take you on a walk through an archeological dig. No games. You won't have to fire any weapons."

Amber shook her head, feeling as though that move unloosed her hair a little. In a metaphorical way. *Let it all fall down.* "Lead on, Captain."

His hand pressed firmly on her shoulder. "Don't worry. I got you. The on switch is right here." He tapped the side of her visor and instantly she stood in a cave. The sudden change in environment made her wobble. "You good?"

"Uh… I think so." She turned her head. It was as though she were surrounded by dark rocky walls and she could see down an aisle that opened into something bigger. "This looks so real." A shiver surprised her. "I almost feel the cool air."

"You do. That's part of the bio-enhanced experience. You don't need to walk, just stand still. If you move your hands, they'll move before you. And… I'm going to join you." Suddenly she could see a man's hand reach out before her. His fingers wiggled. "Our hand-tracking technology is next level. We've overcome self-occlusion and the uncanny valley effect. Try it out. Take my hand."

Always.

She reached out and saw her hand clasp with his and she…felt the warmth of his hand against hers. This was weird! But also incredibly interesting. The reassuring clasp of Val's hand gave her the courage she didn't realize she would need to experience a VR game.

"Do you trust me?" he asked.

Did she? *I want to.* "Lead the way."

Val preferred diving in and going for it. Like leaping out of a plane to free-fall into the Grand Canyon. Or standing in the eye of a hurricane.

But his threshold for excitement and pushing the boundaries was higher than most. Blame it on *inquieto.* He loved to always be in motion. It's what kept him vital. Made him feel alive.

It was always best to start slow for someone who hadn't experienced VR, which is why he hadn't selected a war game for Amber's first run. Verdadero offered a number of exploration games they sold to schools and universities. They simulated actual places such as archaeological digs, underwater diving, a walk through an Egyptian pyramid—even a rainforest search for rare insects.

Amber had tried to hide her reluctance, but he'd sensed it. And not even in her straight posture, which was her norm. It had been in the tone of her voice. She'd needed him to step up, take her hand and guide her.

Soon enough, she let go of his hand and moved forward to explore all the interesting pictographs in the cave. As she stroked a finger over each one, the narrator explained the meaning. Val had the thought that he'd love to get his dad to try one of these walks. Maybe then he'd realize that Verdadero really was doing something good by teaching, and not just putting out shooting games. But how to even convince the old man to step inside Verdadero? He'd never visited the office, no matter how many times Val invited him.

"This is so cool! I can almost feel the mist from that water trickling down the cave wall."

Amber arrived at a short climb and she eagerly jumped over a stream and grasped on to some crevices in the wall. He stood below watching, her feet about level with his chest.

"You're doing well, Amber."

"Yeah?" She glanced down. "Whoa. I don't know. I feel like I'm going to fall."

"You can't physically fall in the game. It's only a simulation. But it may feel—"

He sensed her wobble on the platform beside him before he saw her let go of the rocky handhold in the game. For an inexperienced user, such a move could be terrifying. And they could lose proprioception, an awareness of where their body was.

Tearing off his visor, Val put out his arms to catch Amber as her body faltered and her shoulders swayed backward. He caught her back against his chest, nuzzling his face aside her neck. She smelled so good. No VR game could ever simulate scents. Though, he was working on that.

"Take off the gloves and visor. We're done," he said.

She did so, and still gasping, she turned in his embrace. A wobble set her forward. Crushing her against his chest, he held her in a hug to let her know he was real, that she stood on solid ground and was safe. It was a surreal moment. Many players felt lost and disoriented entering and leaving VR, yet he felt an unprecedented protectiveness toward her.

His fingers tangled in the ends of her curly hair. Softer than he imagined. The heartbeats thundering against his chest prompted him to hug her just a little firmer.

"I'm okay." Her fingers trembled as he took both her hands, unwilling to let her go until she found her bearings. "That was so realistic. I felt like I was falling. My body reacted. You…caught me."

"You wouldn't have gotten hurt in the game."

"I know but…might I have fallen in real life? Landed on the floor?"

Her eyes were so luminous. Trusting, yet worried. He wanted to reassure her that nothing could ever harm her. He'd never felt such a strong protective instinct for a woman before.

She pulled her hands from his and clasped them across her opposite forearms. A shielding move, but also, he suspected, quelling the racing adrenaline.

"It can happen sometimes. That's why this holo-platform is padded." He jumped on the bouncy surface. "You're still all in one piece."

"Thank you. I'm glad you were there to catch

me. You were there." Her eyes brightened with that realization. Too quickly though she shook her head. "But that's enough for me. I got the idea of how VR works."

"I'll take you on a flight to Mars one day."

"I prefer good old terra firma. Whew!" She brushed the hair from her face and turned to look around the room.

Val wanted to hug her again. To feel her warmth and that delicious connection. Her lack of laughter suggested the experience impacted her in ways he should be cautious of. It was that need for control he knew she required. He could recall the first time he'd taken a VR walk. It had always been like flying to him. Something to crave, chase and never stop. Like dancing, but even more exhilarating.

"How about we get a drink in the cafeteria?" he suggested. "Some tea to settle your racing nerves."

"They're not racing," she protested a little too quickly.

"Of course not." She was trying hard not to appear affected. He'd give her that. "But I need some tea. Come on."

Over lemon-ginger tea, Val answered Amber's questions about Verdadero's beginnings. And about his decision to devote his life to coding over dancing.

"You studied flamenco dancing?"

"For years as a teenager. My mother was a professional *bailaora*."

"And how old were you when she died?"

"She passed away when I was seventeen."

"I'm so sorry. It's difficult to lose a parent."

"Do you say that because you've lost one as well?"

"Oh no, I mean, well..." Her posture tightened. "My parents divorced three years ago. After twenty-five years of what I had thought to be a perfect marriage. My mom decided one day she had fulfilled her soul contract with my dad and said it was time to move on to her next experience."

"Interesting."

"But nothing similar to your loss. I've never lost someone close so I can't relate. Should we get back to why you left dance for coding?"

"Of course." Much as he'd enjoy having a deeper conversation with her, Val accepted her gentle guidance to stay on focus. There were questions to be asked, data points to be filled out. "When Teo, Pablo and I created that first game, and saw some success with it, we realized we wanted to go big. I knew I couldn't dance *and* code because there's not enough hours in the day, so I made the choice to set dance aside. And, well, my mother's death made it difficult to want to dance also. As I've explained, giving up dance created the one sore spot between my dad and I. Coding is not something he understands. Flamenco? Now that is what a traditional Spanish son should do, especially since his mother was a dancer."

"Dancing must have bonded the two of you?"

"Oh, yes, I learned everything from my mother. She called me *inquieto*."

"Always on the move?"

"Yes. A jittery bouncer when I was much younger. She taught me to focus that energy into dancing. But I always say I speak three languages. Coding is my first language. Dance is the second, with Spanish a distant third."

"And English as well. You've been very kind to speak English with me."

"Your Spanish is not so good."

She mocked affront, but then laughed. "I do try."

"It is serviceable. It makes Maria laugh."

"Is that so? I'll make a note to brush up. So, the three of you went on to create Verdadero?"

"Yes, the three musketeers. Pablo was the artistic genius behind it all. Teo is the marketer, the salesman, the money man."

"And you provide the code."

"Standing on the holo-platform in the dark room is my happy place."

Amber sipped her tea. "A happy place for you. But not necessarily for any woman who wants to get your attention. You spend more time at work than at home?"

"I do."

"Do you have any desire to balance your work and private life?"

"Balance?" He winced. Sure, he understood what she was asking, but life was more nuanced. He held out his hand and tilted it. "Real-life wobbles, you see? I enjoy working. I don't have to code, but it makes me happy. I want to have a relationship. I want to fall in love. Take you and me. This is nice. Just talking. You're so attentive."

"Lots of people are good listeners."

"Maybe. But I like how you do it. Your body is open and you hold eye contact." He leaned across the table, grabbing her focus. "Do you know people don't even know how to look one another in the eye nowadays?"

"Yes, I've noticed. I suspect it's to do with always having our attention on the screen in our hands. Normally I don't have this tablet with me. I try to avoid screen time when I can. But your life is all about the screen."

"In a manner." It was so much more than a screen with VR. But to begin to explain the intricacies to someone who was more interested in his personal life? Val would not bore her with the tech details. “Hey, you want to duck out and get some *tocino de Cielo*?”

“I have no idea what that is, but the way you say it makes it sound like something I definitely need to check out.”

“It’s a sweet treat. Come on.”

CHAPTER SEVEN

IT LOOKED LIKE FLAN, but apparently it was not. Called *tocino de Cielo*, which translated to *heavenly bacon.* Val explained to Amber that it was called that because of its resemblance to a slice of pork fat.

Weird as it sounded, the caramel custard treat had been delicious. The pastry shop they'd got it from reminded Amber of the Parisian hot spots like Angelina and Ladurée. The place had been packed with tourists so they'd taken their treats to go and now wandered riverside, Val's intention on the electric bike rental spot just ahead.

When he spied the two-seater—side-by-side pedaling—he bounced like an excited kid and gave her a goofy grin. The last time she'd ridden a bike had been in high school. And not that she was out of shape, but sharing the pedaling duty was fine with her, so they rented it and took off for a leisurely ride along the Guadalquivir. He pointed out statues and important buildings, then they strolled through a garden, past a duck pond under the shade of olive and palm trees, and paused at a gazebo.

Amber leaned her elbows on the stone banister. The pond glinted green and gold in the sunlight. Ducks floated in bliss. Some insect chirped. And the air held that ancient scent she couldn't quite place but could feel settle on her skin, as warm and mysterious as a subtle perfume. Or Val's touch. Him holding her on the holo-platform? In the moment she'd been frightened. The experience had felt so real. Only focusing on Val's body heat, his calming voice, had brought her down. And a little too close to desire. She'd quickly stepped back from him.

She regretted that move now. But that regret battled with her need to keep their interactions professional.

"Is this park close to your home?" she asked.

"Not far."

"I would visit daily if I lived nearby. It's idyllic. Does your morning run take you through here?"

"All the time. This scenery reminds me of a masterpiece painting."

"But I thought you liked the moderns?"

"I do, but Verdadero once designed a game for the Louvre. It was an incredible learning experience familiarizing myself with all the artworks."

"I understand a movie is being made of one of your games?"

"For *Matador*, yes. We signed the deal last year. Very exciting."

"Do you get a part in the movie?"

Val laughed. "I didn't think to ask for one. But maybe, eh? That would be something new to try. Though I don't think I should be given a speaking part. I'll stick to the action."

"You do like to move and stay busy."

"Chaos is my calm."

"That's the weirdest thing I've ever heard, but..." That curly hair of his defied taming and sometimes plopped over one mischievous eye. It was all she could do *not* to reach out and flip it aside. "I can see that in you. You've got a lot going on in your life. If you had to slice out something to give you more time to focus on a relationship, what would it be?"

"Is that another question on your assessment?"

It wasn't. And yet, she was here to guide him toward—once a match had been made—*keeping* that match. "I'm curious."

Val leaned his elbows onto the railing beside her and looked over the pond. This easy companionship was a new experience for her. She'd never had a male friend. And her dates were not often spent conversing beyond dinner and discussing the latest Netflix series. Maybe she didn't know how to do small talk? A note to make on her own to-do list if she were ever to someday get serious about her dating life.

"I'm not sure about finding the time," Val offered. "Everything I do is done with purpose and makes me happy. Otherwise, it's a waste of time to do it."

"What about cutting back on your work hours? I think if you had someone in your life, that would be much easier to do than it is to imagine it now."

"You're not wrong. I've watched Teo do that for Cara, who is very important to him. I mean, the two just got married!"

"When was the last time you went on a date? Had a girlfriend?"

"Honestly? My dates are more like one-night stands. And I'm not proud of it."

"There is no shame in ensuring your needs are met." *Speaking for myself.*

"It's not like that. Eh. Sometimes it is. Most of the time it just doesn't feel right so I end it. I don't spend time with someone if it doesn't make me happy."

"Maybe you don't give those one-nighters enough of a chance? To get to know you? For you to get to know them?" Still speaking for—or at—herself? *Oh, Amber. This is not about you.*

"Possible. But I usually suss out quickly if she's just in it for my money. I hate feeling like a lending bank that never asks for repayment on loans."

"I imagine it's difficult what with your bank account. But you must have some specifics you require, because of that money. What is it you want in a woman?"

"No gold diggers. Obviously. I mean, I love to spend money on a woman, but if that's what they're in it for, it makes the gift so much less meaningful. That's why I avoid gifting."

"Flowers are nice." Still speaking for herself! But hey, there were a few simple things in life that appealed to most women. She wasn't going to push away any offering of kindness.

"What I really want is someone to challenge me intellectually." Val turned and leaned his elbows on the balustrade beside her. "And to never stop being curious."

Amber nodded. "I get that. Conversation and sharing experiences."

"It's not so much the words but the connection," Val said. "Resonating with the other person. I can tell if a woman is trying too hard or is attempting to put on an act to be something she's not. I want real."

Could he read her? She tried to remain aloof, a consultant dutifully recording details, but she was finding it difficult not to place herself in this faux dating situation.

On the other hand, she'd decided that was the best way to learn about the man. *So, go Amber!*

"Do you get a lot of women who only see your wallet?" she asked.

He chuckled. "I do. I don't mind that. I have a lot of money. Spending it to make someone happy doesn't bother me. But I'd never buy a person's interest or love."

She recalled the flower he'd pressed into her hair. The moment had felt like some kind of Disney romance scene where the orchestra rose and the feels flowed. "You've a bit of the knight in shining armor in you. You did rescue me in the game."

"A man should never allow a lady to fall. And I mean that metaphorically."

"Oh yeah? What's a metaphorical fall?"

"Like not being looked at as the goddess she is or allowing her to fall from the pedestal."

Amber wrinkled her nose. "Maybe some women don't want to be put on a pedestal."

"You think?"

"I imagine it can be very challenging, even lonely, way up there with the man meeting your every need. We women—some of us, anyway—like to do things for ourselves."

"See, that's what I need to learn. I was raised in a family where the man was the head of the household. He worked. He took care of his family. Women weren't expected to also bring home a paycheck."

"But your mother danced professionally?"

"She danced for a local theater troupe. The pay wasn't much but that wasn't the point. She indulged her creative passions. My dad would have never expected her to contribute to household expenses. Because besides being able to dance she was also the housekeeper, the cook, the caretaker. She did it all and never allowed her dance engagements to get in the way of her taking care of her family. And in turn, my father treated her like the queen she was."

"That's nice. But I think there are a lot of less traditional women nowadays, and today they want to share in the household duties with the man. And the work requirements. Paychecks are validating. We women want it all. Can you get behind that?"

"I can." Not a convincing tone to his voice. With a tilt of his head, he asked, "Can you?"

"It doesn't matter what I like or don't like."

"Yes, it does. What is it you look for in a man?"

Treating her like a date and trying to get to know her better? Very well. She knew how to play this one. "One with a brain and who uses it," she said quickly. Amber shrugged. It was the truth. "Not on socials all the time. Funny. Athletic. Confident. Perfect."

"Perfection is overrated."

"Oh, I don't think so."

"Your standards are high."

"I am driven to succeed. And I'd like a partner who feels the same. I just…want someone who values me."

"I like that. You need to feel valued. Your presence, your emotions, your desires. Everyone needs to know they are accepted."

Those big brown eyes would never stop tugging at her heart. Er—some other woman's heart who would cook for him and kiss him on the cheek when he returned home from work, and who gave him lots of babies. Traditional stuff. It sounded…kind of spectacular.

"Don't get me wrong. I've never been treated terribly by a man," Amber confessed. "I guess I've never truly connected to a man."

"And *you're* a matchmaker?"

"Don't worry. The algorithms do all the work, remember?"

"Good ole algorithms. Still. It's sad that you've never connected to a man."

"Whatever."

"Whatever? Amber, please." He patted a hand over his chest. "You're making my heart break. Don't you want love?"

A sigh hid her need to scream at him that no, she just didn't believe love could last. "My relationships never seem to last long because I'm very…exacting. I like things a certain way. There. You got it out of me. I'm certainly not the woman for most."

"I don't know. I think you need tender loving care. Any man who is worth a morsel of humanity would see that. I like your smile, Amber. You don't wear it often enough." He put up a hand. "And before you protest that men shouldn't be telling women to smile, I get that. I just feel your happiness when you smile. It's genuine."

How to take that compliment without shoving the protest he'd soundly quashed right back at him? "Should we keep pedaling?"

"Let's drop off the bike and we can walk to my villa. It's been a nice afternoon, *sì*?"

"It has. But you haven't worked at all today. Do you need to return to the office?"

"You did say I should spend less time at the office. I'd better start practicing if I'm going to attract a mate. What about dinner out again tonight?"

"Sounds…" *Necessary to get the job done.* "…great. But allow me some time to do a little work once we return to your place?"

"Taking notes on me?"

"That's what you hired me for."

"I was starting to forget that." He got on the

bike, patting the seat beside him. "Your carriage, my lady."

As they pedaled to a bike return, Amber couldn't help think Val was the perfect man for any woman. She'd certainly pick him if she had the opportunity. But that wasn't how Lux Love worked. Val would be matched with a woman in the database.

Of course, Amber was in the database. Her account flagged as an employee so it never accidentally got matched with a client. It was a requirement all employees fill out a survey so they knew what the client experienced. And all the consultants secretly, on occasion, would run their stats against one of the clients. Colette wasn't aware. If she were, there would be a mass firing. Amber had done it twice for her roommates.

Amber couldn't resist wondering how she and Val would match. But the idea of checking scared her. What if they were a terrible match?

Worse yet—what if they matched perfectly? A girl who had lost all trust in love and who wanted to excel in her career trajectory wouldn't want to risk even checking.

CHAPTER EIGHT

UPON ARRIVAL AT the tapas bar, Amber interpreted the Spanish-language sign on the door: No Wi-Fi. Talk to One Another. Tucking her ever-present mini tablet away in her purse, she decided to enter any new details later.

Val walked ahead to the bar as she took in the aged leather and wood furnishings, cozy confines and walls covered with black-and-white photos depicting Sevillian architecture. He'd said to allow him to get her drinks and something to nosh on. She liked that. A take-charge man.

Drawn by the savory scent of seafood and something tomatoey, she joined Val at the bar where he spoke with a couple older men who nursed drinks. They loudly and appreciatively bellowed "Ay!" as she stopped beside Val.

"This is Amber." He introduced her to each of the two men. "Emilio and Homer are permanent fixtures here. If you want to hear the best *cantaor* in all of Seville, here he is."

Emilio bowed his head. *Cantaor* was a singer.

"Nice to meet you both." Amber was about to offer her hand to shake but Val turned and handed her a plate of something, while he took up his own glass and plate.

He nodded toward a back patio that glowed with orange light and echoed out festive clapping. *Palmas?* The clapping that accompanied flamenco dancing.

Sniffing at her drink as she followed him out into a courtyard, she determined the alcohol level could probably run a car for an entire day. Best to eat first before sipping the libations. She was on the clock.

Date number two: Study the man's interactions with others.

A round of cheers greeted them. Amber took in the small courtyard paved with bricks and packed with men and women chatting, nodding, eyeing her. Anxiety level? High. Geeky smart girl so used to getting by on her own and never partying? Mingling and small talk? The horror!

The men clapped Val across the back and, with some, he exchanged cheek kisses. The Spanish did like to touch and make extended eye contact when greeting. Unsettling, but also heartening, if she was honest with herself. Everyone acknowledged her as they made way to a table tucked tightly among others.

"Is this a place you would take a date, Val?"

He slid onto a chair beside her, his elbow nudging hers. Everyone was packed around a small dance floor where a guitarist currently strummed. Behind him on a vine-covered stone wall hung a few more guitars, their wood surfaces faded or worn from decades of strumming.

"Of course. It's my favorite hangout."

"And the obvious next question is…" She wobbled the wine goblet between her fingers. "Do you always ply your dates with strong drinks?"

He smirked and shook his head. "It's orange wine. Locally made. Give it a try."

Amber sipped. Surprisingly sweet, almost honey-like, and it smelled of the orange blossoms that seemed to blanket the city.

"*Vino de naranja*," he said. "Made with oranges grown in my courtyard. It is white wine vinified with the orange peel in an oak barrel. I allow my neighbor to pick my trees clean and he brews small batches."

"You…supply fruit for bootlegger wine?"

"Yes. Maria makes jam with the oranges as well."

"That explains all the preserves in the pantry. So you're an orange supplier, a dancer. *And* you code for a billion-dollar VR gaming company?" Impressive. If not slightly quirky. "What else do you do?"

"Lots of things. I like to keep busy. And I've

got to do something with all the oranges that grow on my property. Warning—never eat the oranges fresh from the tree. They are very bitter. But they make an excellent wine. It roses your cheeks."

Amber touched her cheek. Had she blushed? Had to be the wine.

Val nudged a plate toward her and she took a bite of the crunchy bread. "No, spread the tomato sauce on it and then some salt. You can get messy with it." He took her bread and showed her how to do it. A tiny saltcellar sat on the table, from which he generously sprinkled flakes over the bread. When he handed it to her, the juice from the freshly chopped tomatoes ran down his finger and on to hers.

Caught in his gaze—which, had she a match, might ignite and quickly extinguish to a long and wispy smolder—Amber tugged the bread from him. He licked his finger and winked at her. "Lots of salt is best. Good stuff."

A bite delivered a fresh kick of savory flavors. She wanted to lick her fingers too, but instead grabbed a napkin.

Val leaned an elbow onto the table while his other hand kept a clapping beat on the side of his thigh. A female dancer had taken to the small floor space before the strumming guitarist. She spun, her hips twirling while her head seemed to dart around so quickly it was as if she never took her gaze from the audience. Her expressive hands coiled and glided through the air. The pained look on her wilted-apple face spoke of experiences Amber could not relate to.

"It's a very emotional dance, yes?" she asked.

"Indeed. Steeped with centuries of storytelling. Each song can be traced to a different region and story. I favor the malaguena. It's a fandango style of dance attributed to the Moors. It's a kind of romantic form of the song."

"Is that so? Interesting."

She did understand the romance of flamenco, which included song, dance and the guitarist. There was something so energetic, yet earthy and commanding to it. Mournful, as well.

Someone slapped a hand on Val's shoulder. "Vasquez, you show us how it's done!"

"Ay!" He gave Amber's hand a squeeze as he stood. "I'll be right back."

He did not come right back. And Amber was perfectly fine with that.

The other dancer bowed and gave Val the stage. With a stomp of his foot, he assumed a pose, body stretched, one arm high and hips jutted forward. His head down, he appeared to summon a darkness. A note sung by Emilio wailed painfully, a call to attention. An invitation into that darkness. A cry from someone sitting at a table echoed a distant plea. They were in alliance. A family.

Suddenly, the food didn't matter. As the hairs on Amber's arms stood up, she leaned forward.

Val's first steps beat the small wooden stage while the guitarist's strums accompanied him. An older man sitting on a box drum thumped out a beat matching Val's stomps. While his upper body stayed still, he swished out his arms like a matador, snapping his fingers. His feet were another story, stomping, tapping, beating. A rapid thunder of zapateado. Fierce concentration etched his face. He personified what Amber thought must be the story he told. Angsty and commanding. Wailing yet hopeful.

The man had many talents. Amber didn't see any negatives about him. Besides the unkempt closet. And fine, the lack of a schedule and disregard for time. He seemed kind, vital, polite. Sensual. A part of the very cobbled streets and perfumed air that designed this old city. Authentic with an uncompromising dash toward the future.

All of a sudden he turned slowly, his chin down, arms arced. The fluidity of his body captivated her. Powerful like the bull, yet graceful. A protector who could stand before the bull, swing out the metaphorical cape. He walked in a circle and winked at her before he started a rapid succession of footwork. *Palmas* increased. A few "ays" were shouted. The singer intoned. The guitarist strummed madly.

And then with a final stomp and dust rising about his shoes, Val finished.

Amber's breath gasped out. She pressed a hand over her pounding heart. What a—was she turned on? Her hands felt…sweaty. Her breasts rose with her rapid breaths.

Another woman took Val's place as he returned to sit beside her. His sheepish smile silently asked what she thought of his performance. A little boy looking for validation.

What she wanted to do was grab him by the wrinkled lapel and…kiss him.

Whew! What was that about? Turned on by a man displaying his masculine physique with a few stomps of his feet? Really?

"Amazing," she finally said.

He shrugged, a good-natured dismissal of a wildly incredible talent. One of the elder gentlemen patted Val's shoulder and said something in rapid Spanish. He squatted beside Val's chair and the twosome began to converse.

"Uh…will you excuse me?" Amber wanted to give him the freedom to hold that conversation. And she needed some air. "I need to find something to drink other than wine or I'll be tipsy."

"I'll get you some water?"

"No, you stay. You might be called to dance again. I'll be right back."

As the guitar riffed into rapid fanfare, Amber snuck out of the patio and into the main bar where the air was clearer and she could breathe. It was rare she found herself utterly wordless over a man. Enchanted by his dramatic mating dance.

What was she thinking? He hadn't been trying to seduce her. Well. She'd felt *something* back in that courtyard. She would note that feeling but not on the assessment. That might raise a red flag with the AI.

At the bar she asked for water and the bartender filled a glass with ice.

"You are Senor Vasquez's girlfriend?" The woman handed Amber the water.

"Oh no, I'm vetting—er, his, uh…" It wouldn't be professional to reveal what she was here for. Client privilege. "I'm a lifestyle consultant." Which she was. "Here to…"

"Consult on Val's life?" the bartender guessed.

"A little? He is a bit disorderly."

The bartender laughed. "You've come to bring order to that beautiful mess of a life?" She shook her head and swiped the counter with a cloth. "No, no. You leave him as he is. That man is exactly as he should be."

Interesting. Amber had to ask, "Have you… dated him? I mean, to know that about him?"

"No, I am married, senorita. I just know Val. Everyone in the neighborhood knows Val. He is a passionate man. About everything. You cannot bring order to passion."

Amber might argue differently. Everything needed to be arranged and put in its place. Passion was not necessary to creating such order.

"I'll remember that," she said, to be nice. "Thanks for the water. That orange wine might have put me under the table."

Amber wandered back to the patio doorway where the music had increased intensity. Val sat on his stool, both feet tapping and hands clapping. *Passion, eh?*

Catching sight of her, he smiled and beckoned her over. She couldn't avoid sitting thigh to thigh with him. While clapping, Val leaned in and touched his forehead to hers. A weird intimacy that she didn't want to back away from. And when he leaned back, he smiled. "Is good?"

Oh, yes, he was very good.

CHAPTER NINE

VAL HELD THE front door open for Amber. The night had chilled and she'd been glad she had worn a sweater, cropped as it was. As they entered his villa, he heard the faint tones of a malaguena echoing out from the kitchen. It was after midnight. Had Maria left her TV on before turning in? Sometimes the housekeeper did stay up late making bread. Yes, he smelled the yeast.

Before Amber could turn down the hallway toward the guest room, he stomped a few *golpes* and took her hand, walking her toward the inner courtyard. "Dance with me, Senorita!"

She tugged from his grasp. "Oh, I'm not a dancer."

No, but she didn't have to know the steps to move her body. Tension seemed to be the woman's natural mien. She needed to shake her lush curls and allow her muscles to relax. To feel her body as only dance would allow.

He stepped in time to the faint music, back arched proudly as a dancer must display. Performing some measured heel-toe walks, he approached her with a hint of defiance. A glowering look that was supposed to display the grief of his ancestors but—eh, it probably looked a bit threatening so he abandoned it. “Anyone can dance. It is a way to get to know your body, *sì*?”

She shook her head. Rubbed a palm up one arm. Shy? He wouldn’t press. But he wasn’t ready to let her walk away from him. Sitting so close to her on the patio, feeling her body heat, inhaling her spicy citrus scent, there was no way he’d get her out of his senses. And he wasn’t sure he wanted to.

“Flamenco is a lifestyle,” he said. “It is said the *cante* or *bailaor* cannot perform without immersing themselves in the beat, the compas.” He patted his chest over his heart. “It is all about the compas.”

He walked purposefully around her, snapping his fingers *contratiempo* to show her the beat that he no longer heard from the kitchen. It now ran through his veins.

“Flamenco *is* a very sexy dance,” she offered.

“You say so?” An easy smile boosted Val’s confidence, the matador standing before a not-so-threatening bull. “Flamenco is *passion*.”

“Right. I did hear someone say you were passionate tonight.”

He did possess a passion for movement, telling a story, and entering the state where dance fused with emotion and his very atoms.

Val bowed his head and looked through his lashes at her. “One must rouse the daemon to truly dance as our ancestors danced.”

“The daemon?”

“Duende.” He calmly walked around her, studying the tightness of her shoulders. He didn’t want her fearful of him, but he did want to see if she would soften, lean into his presence. The dance. The daemon within him.

Or just…smile at him. Give him some signal she wasn’t offended by him. And that their interactions weren’t all work for her. Did she never relent with her mental note taking? How to see inside the woman? To bridge the work side of Amber Martin to the personal side. Curiosity nudged at him.

“Walk slowly,” he instructed. “Keep your eyes on mine.”

She looked at him then quickly averted her gaze. A matchmaker who played it coy? Interesting. Also, he couldn’t have that. Val snapped his fingers in *pitos* before her, bringing his elbows up and his hands out to direct her gaze, slowly, eventually, up to his eyes. He smiled at her, softening his stance. She tugged in her lower lip with her teeth.

“The *rosas* is the slower more serious part of

the dance." He slowed his pace, his shoes brushing the tile floor. "It is a moment to take in your breath and touch your daemon. Thank it."

"Thank it?" She hadn't dropped his gaze. Her attentiveness turned him on. It softened her stuffy professional side. And made it easier for him to relate. They inhabited his realm now. The safety of flamenco.

"Thank the daemon for the dance. It is what keeps me vital." He finished with a short zapateado and then stomped the ground with both feet. "Olé!"

Out the corner of his eye, he noticed movement in the kitchen. Maria had slipped back from watching them. Val chuckled and ran his fingers through his hair. "I do love to dance."

Amber pressed a hand to her chest. Bewildered? "Whoever matches with you will have to love flamenco."

"That would be a good quality. Tell me, do you love flamenco?"

"It's incredible. I could watch it every day. Especially the way you move—oh." She stepped back from him. Finding her self-assigned place. Protecting a part of herself that he wanted to delve into. No longer under the spell of his daemon.

She fluttered her hand before her. "Boy, it's getting late, yes?"

It wasn't too late to kiss her. Val studied her expression. Teeth worrying at her teasing red lip. Eyes darting. She couldn't hold his gaze for more than a moment. He wanted her to look at him. To touch him as he touched her. Absently. Reassuringly. Kindly. Testing.

"Val?"

"Huh? Yes." He'd lost himself. In something that fascinated him. "Did you get more information for your assessment tonight?"

"I did. And I'll want to fill that out before turning in. Thank you for being so kind with your time, Val. I know you could be working instead of entertaining me."

"It is important to spend time with you."

"For the matchmaking," she said.

"Yes. For the matchmaking." And for himself. Because he'd not spent such a satisfying evening with a woman in a long time. He liked how he felt when with Amber. Without that tablet in her hand. "We should probably go on a few more dates, *sì*? So you can establish a thorough understanding of…who I am?"

"Feels…necessary."

He stepped closer to her. "It does."

Brown eyes. Soft. Liquid. Unsure. If he touched her, ran a thumb along her jaw and cupped the back of her head, he'd have to kiss her. Stake a claim to her lush red mouth.

Every molecule of his being swayed his hand upward…

"So good night then." Amber backed away, turned and rushed down the hallway.

Val clasped his fingers in a soft clench, so close to having touched her. Had he done something wrong? For her to flee?

Of course. He'd been treating her like a date, a woman he was interested in. She was a consultant, not someone he should look at in any way other than as a business relationship.

That was growing more difficult day by day.

CHAPTER TEN

AMBER ANSWERED THE call from her boss, Colette. "How's it progressing with Senor Vasquez? It looks like his profile is filling in nicely."

As usual, Val had left for work by the time she had risen this morning.

"It's going well. I've been on a few dates with him so I can observe his mannerisms and the way he treats a woman. Such a gentleman. And a very talented dancer."

Oh, that dance last night. If she'd been unsettled watching him dance at the bar among so many others, that private dance in the courtyard had taken her beyond…something. Why could she not place the feelings? She'd been around sexy men before. Could appreciate them for their looks and charm. But Val went beyond surface appeal. He fascinated her on a visceral level. Not sexual but, yes, she had found herself getting aroused. Had she never been seduced by a man before? Why did this feel so new? So…desirable.

Not that he'd been trying to seduce her.

Or had he?

"Remember the golden rule, Amber," Colette said. "Don't fall in love."

"You keep saying that, but I know you hired me because of my miserable dating history."

"I do recall you saying you loved love for other people but didn't need it for yourself. I don't want to begin to examine that statement. And you do have a certain astute detachment from emotion that I think works well for this job. But don't allow that to keep you from seeing into the client's heart. A consultant must dig deep."

"Of course."

Detached from emotion? Her? Check. Unless a sexy man danced a private flamenco before her. He may have almost kissed her last night. Why hadn't she let it happen?

Because she was a professional.

"Don't worry, Colette. Val is a remarkable man but my detachment from emotion won't keep me from digging deep into his emotional needs and values."

Colette's chuckle brandished an edge of disbelief that made Amber question her own words. Really? *Was* she attracted to Valentino Vasquez? She merely appreciated a man who checked off all the admirable qualities on the database. Any woman would be!

"It's been days," Colette said. "We need to set

up the client with a date soon. But you must fill in the client's wants section. What does he want in a woman? Her looks, her career, her personal motivations? If you get that filled in, Amber, then we can start generating a search."

"Of course." She'd learned some of that already but had yet to enter it in the database. "I'll make sure it's completed today."

"Get on it, Amber. Report back tomorrow!"

"I will. *Merci*, Colette."

Amber clicked off and set her phone aside on the bench. She sat in the courtyard, shoes kicked off and feet nestled in the cool grass beneath the canopy of verdant leaves. Untethered by the breeze, orange blossom petals rained down. It was a heavenly spot. Grounding. Not something she would have ever tried in her lifetime. She intended to make bare feet in the grass a new habit.

Colette was already pushing for Val's first date? She really did need to step up and get that wants section completed.

She checked the time. It wasn't even noon. Would it be too forward to show up at his work with lunch? Probably. But she wasn't trying to pick up a rich man and stuff him in her pocket. She had a job to do. And he had been informed that conversations with Lux Love's consultant were part of the process.

With a decisive nod, she decided to stop by a

restaurant for takeaway on the way to Val's office. She wouldn't bother Maria to cook. That woman… Nonnegotiable? Val really did need to hire a housekeeper. Who knew how to use a vacuum. And operate a washing machine.

Val set his visor aside and leaned back in the chair. The massage rollers gently eased his lumbar region while the body sensors read his biorhythms.

Blowing out a breath and shoving his fingers through his hair, he shook his head. He'd been working on the same line of code for fifteen minutes. Wasn't even seeing the letters and numbers anymore because all he could see were Amber's bright eyes. Those sensual red lips. Tugged by a white tooth when uncertain. And that look of interest she'd held as she'd watched him dance around her last night.

Maybe he wielded some charm in his arsenal after all? Pablo would be proud his buddy could loosen up in a woman's presence. And sure, he wasn't a total dweeb around women. To his surprise, he'd learned money softened his anxiety. Throw it around and that alleviated any nervous uncertainty on a date. It was just when he sought meaningful connections that he froze up. Emotional unions? That sucked away his confidence and reduced him to that awkward schoolboy all over again.

So he'd gotten what he'd put out regarding relationships. Surface-level experiences. Women attracted to what he could give them. Trips, jewels, Vespas. That was all so surface. His soul craved something different. Something real.

He rarely found himself daydreaming about a woman unless he was attracted to her. Amber made him look away from his work. He was so eager to see her that he wanted to go home immediately to spend time with her. Because once his match was found, Amber would leave. Or sooner. Apparently, the consultant walked away as soon as dates began. After she recorded every minute detail of his life and…

He had to chuckle to think of the lifestyle changes she'd suggested for him. Hire a new housekeeper? Not going to happen. Less work?

He liked to stay busy. It helped him avoid taking care of himself. He paid others to feed and clothe him. To schedule his life. To entertain him. No time. No desire. But that wasn't what he wanted to be. He should be in control of his own life.

He *could* work less. He didn't need to spend all day here at the office. Once upon a time he'd lived a balanced life; now, he was essentially a recluse. The more his father had pushed his son to find a wife and begin a family, the more Val had shoved back. He would not be told what to do!

Until he'd realized maybe it was time to start looking to his personal life. At thirty-two, he wasn't getting any younger. He didn't need to code all the games. He didn't even need to check the work of his fellow coders. They were talented. As skilled as he was in coding. He rarely caught errors. And if he missed them? Hal would find them.

Could his lack of perspective, stemming from being confined to this room, have been the cause for his unfulfilled life? Didn't he deserve a happy life? A family? Why did he feel as though he *didn't* deserve that?

It had nothing to do with Pablo being struck down so young and never getting to experience creating his own family. Maybe a small part of it was that. Had his mother's death given him cause to push away dance and anything that gave him a spark of happiness? It had for a while.

Coding was happiness when he didn't do it all day every day.

A man really needed to get away from this chair, communicate with those around him. Live. Allow some balance into his life yet still be able to wobble at will.

He did deserve a good life. And listening to Amber talk about his talents and attributes that would attract a woman gave him hope it was possible. And if that woman were like Amber? Smart, witty, easy to talk to. Their conversations were insightful. He enjoyed that. She did tend to pull back, keep to their business relationship when they went too deep, though. Expected. And she had to control the situation, he'd felt that too. This was her first time as a matchmaker? She was doing well.

They had more in common than not. Both geeky and slightly unsure about social mannerisms. He couldn't stop thinking about kissing Amber when she stood close and he watched her lips move as she talked. The woman…needed to be held. To be cherished. To be kissed soundly.

A knock at his dark room door startled him up from the chair. He commanded Hal to unlock and open it and there stood the woman of his daydreams. "Amber?"

She held up a brown bag. "I brought lunch. I suspect you may not have taken a break?"

"You suspect correctly. What's in there? It smells great."

"It's paella. I've never had the authentic Spanish version. It smells ridiculously yummy."

"You picked my favorite meal." He took the bag from her, kissed both of her cheeks—this time she did not pull away as if startled—then led her down the hallway. “We’ll lunch in my office. I don’t like to have food in the dark room.”

“Sounds good. Have you seriously been in this room since dawn?”

“I have.” That answer was beginning to make him feel guilty. He opened his office door and gestured she enter. “Was just thinking about…”

Amber. His heart rate was really zooming now. Good thing Hal wasn’t connected to this office or the AI would suggest he reduce his stress.

“Yes?” she prompted. “What were you thinking about?”

“Uh, how I do need to cut down on my work hours?”

“Are you telling me or asking me?”

He caught her smile. “Do you think a man can change his ingrained habits?”

She arranged food containers and utensils on his empty desktop. “I’m not sure. I have habits that probably need changing. I also work too hard. Won’t ask for help. I’m always trying to prove myself. If I don’t get a gold star then I feel I’ve failed.”

“I get that. A tiny bit of foiled paper. Gold stars, real or implied, make a person feel valued. Isn’t that crazy? Our worth is directly related to our achievements.”

She sighed. “To hear it put that way is a little sad. This one’s yours.” She pushed a takeaway box toward him. "I went with a version without seafood. I've never tried shrimp, believe it or not."

Val took the food box and then…he switched his with hers. She gaped at him. He shrugged. "Let's change up our routines, eh?"

She gave a little agreeing shoulder wiggle, fetched his box and sat opposite him at his desk. "Here goes nothing."

"Nothing doesn't really exist." He marveled over the rich saffron rice. "It's either a one or a zero."

"Isn't zero nothing?"

"Do you really want to get into this conversation?" He forked in some paella. "It's geek stuff."

"I have an idea of where it leads. Something about an absence of quantity?"

"Very good. And you must actually have nothing before you can assign the value of zero to it—yes, I recognize that glazed look in your eyes. I won't go into the mathematical weeds."

"Thank you. But keep talking about the stuff you are passionate about. It's relaxing to listen to your voice."

"It is?"

She laughed. "Sort of? It's very calm and sure. You are confident in body and your surroundings."

He was. Despite his belief he was not. But that

she'd pointed it out made him relax a little more. It was easy being with Amber.

"Actually, I came by to pick your brain again."

"Haven't you mined everything out of it already?"

"If I took out everything, wouldn't nothing be left?" A lift of one of her brows challenged him.

"There would still be a hunk of matter that weighs approximately three pounds jiggling up here." He shook his head. "Still computing, still creating my passion."

"Yes, passion. Like your dancing?"

"Coding makes me passionate as well. It's not as dramatic as flamenco. But I still need to mine the daemon for coding on occasion."

She propped an elbow on the table and rested her chin on the back of her hand. "How so?"

"There is a story to all of the games we create at Verdadero. Emotion, drama, conflict, passion. It requires one mine deep."

"Even for ones and zeros?"

"Even so. Those ones and zeros must allow the player to feel and experience the game as if it were really happening to them."

Amber sat back. "Do you think someday people will sit around in their homes, VR goggles on all day as they experience things they can only dream of?"

"It's a possibility."

"Ugh. I hope not. I was replaced at the law firm by AI."

"Law firm? How come I didn't know that about you?"

"Because you didn't ask? Before landing the Lux Love job I was a paralegal. I'm a research addict. Turns out when it comes to research skills, AI is excellent and cheap. So...bye, bye, Amber."

"I'm sorry. We believe AI will take over the boring, mindless jobs that humans would rather not do, but there is validation in having a job and doing meaningful work."

"Yes, the gold star."

"So with a background in legal research, how did you land in matchmaking?"

"My aunt knows my boss. And she knew I wanted to travel. She put in a good word for me, and Colette took a chance on me."

"Matchmaking in Paris. That's almost a cliché in the romance department, isn't it? Yet you've indicated you're not a big believer in love?"

"I believe in love. I just—" she gave it some thought "—don't have high hopes it can persist. My best example of love was my parents' marriage. After twenty-five years they divorced. So..."

"Hey, at least they had the twenty-five years to learn and grow together."

"You're optimistically pragmatic. I find your

background and desire for the traditional fascinating, yet you also live a fast-paced lifestyle that focuses on the future and technology. You're a dichotomy. In a good way."

"I'll take that as a compliment. You are as well."

"How so?"

"Doesn't believe in love yet she's fixing up people in love matches."

"I'm not doing the actual fixing up. I'm just filling out the assessment. It's all in the nonexistent hands of the AI. Of which, I certainly hope AI doesn't overstep and start moving in on romance."

"Too late. The AI companions available right now are designed to simulate real-life friendships and relationships."

"That's terrible!"

"Perhaps Lux Love will be matchmaking humans to AI sims some day?"

"Never!" She laughed at her passionate reply. "Sorry. I don't ever want to live in that world."

"Same. But it's a generational thing. Young people nowadays will be much less averse to the idea of a robot as a partner than you and I are. Still. I don't think a person will ever be able to exchange meaningful looks with a robotic companion. Just look at it as a helpful assistant."

Her eyes latched to his. He could look into hers

all day. Sense her soft breaths, the subtle orange perfume lingering on her skin.

"Right," she said slowly, touching her lips. "And forget physical touch from some sort of robotic being. It could never be so gentle."

"Oh, it could. But no." Val quickly added, "No robot romance."

"I agree." Her mouth revealed her thoughts before she spoke them. That subtle tooth pull. Parted and expecting lips. Wanting. He could reach—

Amber shook her head. Val lost the enchantment.

"So back to your wants," she said. "You're open on the career front as well. How about personality?"

He'd been so close to touching her. Making contact. Probably for the best?

"You mean like giggly and fun as opposed to serious and exacting?"

She straightened her shoulders. She did swing from relaxed to serious in the snap of a finger. As shifting in her emotions as he supposed he was. But he tended more toward, hmm…passion.

Really, it was duende. Two souls dancing around one another with words and subtle expressions. It was that untamable something he needed and craved.

Val leaned forward, pushing his takeaway box

aside. "I like a well-rounded personality. Someone who can have fun, likes to talk, but isn't an airhead and—if we're going to be real here, I'm not keen on someone who lives for shopping and being seen. You know, like those influencers whose lives revolve around getting likes and follows? Always with a phone recording their every experience. I want someone with whom I can converse."

"I agree," she said softly.

Had she fallen into his accidental enchantment again? What to do? Dare he kiss her? It…didn't feel right. She was wobbly. Off-balance. And he liked that, but he knew she did not. She needed to stay in control.

"No influencers," she noted with a dash across her tablet. "But what if you matched to one?"

"How could I? If you enter my wants in the database, the algorithms will do their job."

"You and your algorithms."

"I trust them completely. I mean, it all traces back to the original programmer, right? The AI is only as smart as the person coding it, feeding it the information. But I did my research on Lux Love. Your success rate is impressive."

"We are very thorough."

Struck by a sudden desire, Val leaned forward. "Are *you* in the database?"

"I am."

"Really?" He sat up straight.

"But we're not allowed to be included in searches. We fill out a profile to know what the clients' side of the experience looks like. Moving on..."

He didn't want to move on. He wanted to hack into Lux Love and put Amber in the search database for his match.

"Tell me about some of your past girlfriends?" The woman was certainly focused.

"Why? You want to dissect why the relationships didn't work out?"

She lifted her shoulders. "It can be helpful. Learning from one's past mistakes."

"You going to eat that?"

She forked a few pieces of shrimp into his box. "They taste great but I'm not as hungry as I thought I was. What about your mushrooms?" He pushed his box toward her so she could fork them out. "Thanks. So how many women have you dated seriously?"

"Seriously? Like more than a few months? One or two. Lots of one-nighters, weeklong hookups, things like that."

"What was your longest relationship?"

"Six months. About a year into university. I really loved her. Or I thought I did." Val set the box on the desk to give her his complete attention. "What even is love?"

"Right?" Amber leaned her elbows onto the table and caught her cheek against her hand. "It's hard to define. Numbers and bits and bytes are great, but ultimately, it's a soul deep thing, don't you think?"

"Possibly. Do you think your parents were soulmates?"

"Oh." Her wince alerted him the topic was touchy for her.

"I mean, parents aside, do you think there is a specific soul out there designed for one other soul?"

"I've never thought much about it, but I like that. Unless you count watching movies with princesses who find their prince charming. Doesn't everyone want that? But then again, love does have an expiration date. So…"

Her parents' divorce had worked a number on her. Val could relate. He'd given up dance following his mother's death. Heavy events like that tended to change a person's way of thinking. But he hated to think that Amber might never allow herself the freedom to open her heart when love stepped up.

"Have you ever been in love?" he asked.

Amber shook her head. "I don't think so. I've had boyfriends but they always…" She winced. "I don't like to risk intimacy with someone I don't know. I've never been with a man where I felt I could walk around naked and just…be."

He wanted to undress her. Touch all of her to see how she reacted. Would her back arch if he touched her stomach? Would a stroke along her throat make her sigh?

"*That's* your criteria? Being naked and comfortable?"

She shrugged. "It's a start, isn't it?"

"Interesting. There's the thrill of new love and being with someone but it gets old fast if all you share is sex."

"Right? Whatever happened to slow walks and holding hands?"

"I love holding hands."

"I've noticed you are a toucher. You like to make contact."

"Anything wrong with that?"

"Not at all."

"Listen. I know I'm a workaholic. That's usually the deal-breaker with my dates and girlfriends. I can't commit or find the time."

"You'd find the time if she was the right person for you. Work would slip your mind like scheduling appointments on your calendar slips your mind."

"Probably." He poked at his remaining paella. "So, if I catch you walking naked through my villa, does that mean you're comfortable with me?"

She laughed and choked a little on a bite of food. "Not going to happen. I don't think my boss would approve."

"*Sì*, but I would."

Amber's jaw dropped open, mid-chew. He'd caught her out.

Sitting back, she closed the lid of her empty meal container and set it in the takeaway bag. "Ahem. Back to the assessment. I like that you seem open to anything."

Val splayed out a hand. "I'm very adaptable and eager to be matched to most any woman. And I promise I will be fully dressed our first meeting."

"Good call. Not that your abs wouldn't serve as a perfect conversation starter."

Heh. So he'd made an impression on her that first night? She wasn't so staunch and emotionless as she tried to convey.

"I, uh, suspect we'll have a match for you soon after I've entered this info."

"Any more details you need on my preferences?"

"I assume your values should match the woman's. Trust, honesty, humor, loyalty. Anything else important? Why *did* you break it off with those two longer relationships? It wasn't just because of your work habits, was it?"

"One didn't want to get married, but she did want me to buy her a flat in Paris."

"A gold digger?"

"Yes, that's what you call it. And the other was…well, I imagined myself married to her. And we even talked about it one night."

"That's serious."

"It was. But she—no, it was me. Ultimately, I was scared to dive in. To step away from this singular life I have. It's a good life. I can do what I want, when I want, and don't have to answer to anyone."

"So why suddenly do you feel the need to settle down? You said something about your dad wanting a traditional marriage for you. You're smart enough to know you can't please others. Most especially family."

"I am smart. As are you. You know things about me even I have to give some thought to. No, contacting Lux Love for a match was not completely because of my dad's wishes. Honestly? I realized such an attitude of not wanting to answer to anyone was selfish. And not my true values. Teo changed when he fell in love with Cara last year. Not that he wasn't a good man to begin with, but a light sparked in his eyes. He became more…buoyant. Bright. I want that light. Does that sound silly?"

"That sounds downright romantic."

"*Sì?*"

Amber clasped her hands on her lap and nodded, not meeting his gaze. "Lux Love will bring that buoyant brightness to your life. Promise."

Not selling it with her posture. Then again, she was Miss Impossible regarding love.

Dare he brainstorm how to get *her* profile activated at Lux Love?

CHAPTER ELEVEN

THE MOVERS LEFT after completing their task. Amber had called them. Another night with that bull's head staring at her was not conducive to a good night's rest. When she'd consulted with Val via text where to put it, he'd said "Wherever," that he'd didn't care.

Really? The man needed to be more involved in—well, everything in his life. He was too lackadaisical at times. So, now Amber stood in Val's bedroom. Staring at the bull's head on the wall. Was she taking this a little too far? Honestly? The bedroom was sparsely furnished with a massive king-size bed on a wood platform, and but a single square wood block as a nightstand for a lamp. No paintings, no decorations. It looked great on the wall. Gave the room gravitas. But it wasn't something she could imagine Val's future wife would enjoy staring at.

With a secret smile of success, Amber turned off the lights and left the bedroom. Not sabotage, she argued inwardly. Just…a welcome gift to his match.

By the time she landed in the kitchen, doubt attacked. What had she just done? Was she allowing emotions to hinder her work? That was a very personal move she'd just made. It screamed *jealousy* in a manner she couldn't quite figure out. She'd never been jealous before. And of a nonexistent woman, at that!

Grabbing a coconut water from the fridge, Amber shook her head at her inner argument. It would be fine. She'd done nothing wrong. In fact, she'd enhanced the decor of the man's room.

Maria eyed her and said something she almost thought sounded like a curse. In… English.

Amber narrowed her gaze on Maria. The housekeeper lifted her head and resumed placing groceries that had been delivered inside the pantry.

"Sure, whatever." Amber strolled outside. She didn't notice Maria's sudden twist of head to look over her shoulder at her.

Val managed an evening away from the office. If he didn't spend time with Amber now, he might regret it. She would leave as soon as the computer spit out his first match. So he suggested a movie night and she eagerly accepted. That both bolstered his confidence and made him realize that maybe making time for someone else wasn't such a challenge. And the reward was far greater than perfectly vibed code.

The inner courtyard was private and lush. Val had the stone hearth installed when he had moved in. When he entertained, which was rare of late, his chef made fire-grilled pizzas and unique smoked drinks for his friends.

Now a low fire crackled. Amber gathered the takeaway boxes from the supper they'd just eaten, and when she asked if he wanted a beer from the kitchen, he said yes.

He stoked the fire and settled on the rug, leaning against the cushioned front of a big cozy sofa. The open courtyard looked up to that big azure sky he'd loved all his life. Stars twinkled. Everything felt ripe for romance.

And he was just daring enough to see if it might happen.

The night was sultry, even though the temperature had sunk. Her cashmere shrug had been a lifesaver for the cool spring evenings here in Seville. Amber soaked in the warmth from the fire, the lingering *azahar* perfume kissed with a hint of fire flame. Orange wine warmed her throat and loosened her muscles. She and Val sat on a huge woven rug before the fire, leaning against the sofa, looking up to the sky where the full moon was framed by the tops of two orange trees.

Everything about this evening felt unreal to her. From the luxurious courtyard and food delivered by a driverless car, to the heady star-kissed atmosphere, to the handsome man sitting so close their arms rubbed. And when he laughed at her story about getting lost on the metro for three hours when she'd first arrived in Paris, his hair had fallen over his eyes and she'd swept it away. One quick dash of her fingers.

Now a sneak glance found Val's eyes closed, head tilted back as if moon bathing. She'd not witnessed him embody such stillness. So there was a calm within the beautiful chaos. Had she unearthed that?

She'd take the credit, but only because she was feeling rather chuffed by her success with the man. And she would call it a success. Sure, the assessment was almost completed. But it was the gentle suggestions to change she had made that he'd taken to heart. Taking time off work? Check. Talking about himself on dates? Check. And the foyer had even been straightened of the mess. Had he asked Maria to do that? She hadn't noticed a cleaning woman checking in.

Colette should be pleased. Amber would ensure this eligible billionaire bachelor would be matched.

Here's looking to a nice commission for a job well done.

And she hadn't fallen in love.

For the most part.

"Hey, do you want to watch a movie?" Val suddenly asked. He tapped his watch and with a click, a large screen lowered from an overhang she'd thought simply part of the architecture. "Cool, right? Ever since I was a little boy in Triana I've always wanted one of these fancy hidden screens."

"Impressive. What movie are you thinking?"

"And oldie, for sure. I'll bring up the list and you can pick."

"Fair enough."

As he tapped away, she studied his grin. Innocent in that little-boy-who'd-earned-the-toy manner, but also so attractive.

How could a woman—any woman—not fall a little bit in love with the adorable tech CEO? There was something about the man that *tugged* at her. Something deep within that she couldn't name or place. He'd grasped hold of it and—

And really, if *she* didn't fall in love with him then who else would? Such feelings indicated she had a winner. Any woman could fall in love with him.

Maybe she was on to something here? Had Colette overlooked that tiny detail? The client should be lovable! So if a consultant responded to the lovable parts of their client, then excellent.

She wasn't going to overthink her logic. She'd learned who Valentino Vasquez was and she adored him.

"Which one?" he asked.

She scanned the list on the screen. "Of course, *My Fair Lady*."

"Love it. *Words! Words! I'm so sick of words!*"

"*I get words all day through*." She continued the lyrics of what was one of her favorite songs in the show. The woman in the movie was so over pretty words from her gentleman callers. All she wanted was for them to show her that they cared for her, hungered for her…

It wasn't an empty sentiment. Any woman would want as much.

The movie began. The warm touch of Val's hand slid against her palm. She closed her eyes as their fingers entangled.

"I know what your love language is," she said.

"Yeah?"

"Touch. You like to make contact. Always. It's nice."

"Touch." He squeezed her hand. "I think you're right. What's your love language? Perfection?"

It hurt to hear that word because it sounded judgmental and foolish now. "No, I think it's…" *Not pretty words.* "…being seen."

"I see you."

She turned to meet his gaze. Always, a smile in his irises. And that seductive darkness. "Yes, you really do."

As they settled to watch the movie, Amber didn't pull her hand from Val's. And she didn't even think of the impropriety because throughout the movie they parted as each broke into song. At one point Val went to the kitchen to retrieve another beer for each of them and he returned doing a little dance to Professor Higgins's song. And as the credits rolled, their shoulders hugged, and Amber's head tilted against Val's.

Val stirred subtly. His dark brown irises danced across her face. His smile assumed charm mode. With a shy bow of his head, he then caught her stare again and said, "I want to kiss you."

Oh. Oh?

No. That…

Was exactly what she wanted.

He turned his body to face hers. "That's all I've been thinking about since Professor Higgins realized he's grown accustomed to Eliza's face. I've grown accustomed to your face, Amber. Your lips. Your mouth. Would a kiss taste like orange wine?"

"Val—"

"It's touch, Amber. My love language."

"Yes, but I'm working for you." Seemed the

appropriate response for a professional matchmaker who must *never* fall in love with her client.

On the other hand, she had gleefully sung through an entire movie alongside him, batting her lashes during the cheeky parts, and sighing dramatically at the sad ones. And it hadn't at all been related to learning more about him for his profile.

Why was she forcing herself to resist something that felt real? Meant to be?

Because you want to show your boss you are capable and worth being promoted to a full-time consultant. Because you think that love can't be real? Or last? What if she did open up her heart to Val only to have her world and her heart crushed when finally, he was matched with a client?

All of it was too risky.

"We are adults, Amber. And I get that I am your client. But right now? We're just two people sitting under the moonlight, acting out one of the best movies ever made. I assumed this was a nonwork thing."

He leaned in closer, his eyes tracing her mouth with seductive scrutiny. She tugged in her lower lip. Touch? *Yes, please.*

"If you don't want a kiss," he whispered, "just say *no*."

When had a *yes* or *no* question been so difficult to respond to?

Amber struggled inwardly with the right and wrong of it. Her astute professional career girl screamed that she'd be messing up any chance of keeping the consultant position and ultimately paying off her credit card bills. While the softer, deeply guarded part of her reached out and made a gimme gesture with her fingers. She was so needy. Wanted real intimacy. With a man who related to her on a level she'd never experienced. He got her.

What was wrong with one little kiss? No one had to know. And really, it wouldn't equal insta-love to be eventually quashed by a breakup.

"Haven't you thought about kissing me?"

Yes! But not falling in love with the billionaire.

But again, not that a kiss required love…

"I will add," Val said on a breathy tone that seemed to mine deep from within his soul, "that no response will be taken as an affirmative."

Amber swore inwardly. She wanted this kiss. She wanted him to take her in his arms and… ravish her. She wasn't even sure what ravishing involved. But oh, did it feel acceptable.

"Very well." Val leaned closer. "No response. That means…"

She didn't flinch as his head moved closer. His eyes focused on her lips, which she parted, because a gasp was unavoidable. That hush of breath countered her rushing heartbeats. The flames crackling beside them played harmony to the electricity zinging through her veins. Ultra-alert, her skin prickled, growing receptive as his breath hushed over her lips.

Push him away!

The professional part of Amber Martin was just too much. Too perfectionist. Too people-pleasing. Too resistant to the emotions striving for release. For once in her life, she had to abandon the quest for seeking approval from others.

Or she'd never know the touch of Val's kiss.

Amber slid her hand along his neck and pulled him against her mouth. His hand cupped the back of her head. The kiss, hard and seeking, crushed and then did not, and then it sought again. Combustible as the flames. As grounding as a flamenco dancer's feet beating the earth. They clung to one another, chasing heartbeats and gasping sighs. Their urgency found a rhythm. Slower, but tight and insistent. He tasted like the local craft beer they'd been drinking. And his hard body against hers tempted her to arch her back, slide up a leg along his to feel all of him, as much of him as she could discover.

Because this kiss was an anomaly. It could never happen again. So she'd enjoy it while she could.

The kiss alternated between hunger and a slower exploration. Val's hand slid along her arm, and then against her rib cage, holding her. His thumb pressed up under her breast. A subtle connection that did not-so-subtle things to her body. They didn't part. How to force apart the north from the south? Yet, they weren't so much like opposites poles. She could geek out with him at the best of times.

Stop thinking, Amber.

This wasn't love. This was passion. What was that word he'd used? *Duende*. It was stirred in a mix of wanting, knowing and expressing that passion between one another. Sometimes a girl had to brush off her exterior armor and let the arrow pierce her softness. Because Amber had a softness that craved this moment. Despite the risk.

Val ended the kiss. Bowed his forehead to hers. Always connecting to her, skin to skin. "Had to do that."

He didn't say sorry. That word might have cruelly ripped out the arrow. For now, Amber wanted to leave it in. A love dart, of sorts. "I should…" Leave? What was she thinking? Now that she did start to think, practicality and propriety began to grip that arrow by the shaft…

As Val bowed his head to hers, she knew what was coming and—*push him away!*

Amber gripped Val's shirt lapel and pulled him to her mouth. She kissed him quickly. Once. Twice. But as the angel and devil struggled in a fistfight on her shoulder, she grasped some modicum of sanity, and pushed away from his delicious mouth.

Now that they'd kissed, things were beginning to click inside her. Things she'd never felt click before. And that was not a metaphor. Yes, arousal, but it was something beyond that. A weird sort of…knowing?

Had they begun something tonight?

No one would have to know. It wasn't as though Colette could see through the tablet and watch Amber's every move. Unless—no, she knew the camera on the tablet was only front facing.

So, yes. She'd kissed the client.

And she'd liked it.

CHAPTER TWELVE

AMBER WOKE TO a message from Lux Love. A 92 percent match had been found for Val. The woman, Carmen Alonso, even lived in Seville. A recruiter for a global charity organization, she traveled for her job and was leaving in three days for Ecuador. Would it be possible to set up a date soon?

Amber replied that it would happen. She'd report back with details later.

Tossing her phone aside, she knew she'd have to call Val because he was likely at work. Probably had been there for hours.

She traced her lips. Was he thinking of last night's kiss under the moonlight?

Why had she let that happen? It had been the most exciting, intoxicating, titillating—she ran out of adjectives. It had rocked her world.

And now Carmen, who was a freakin' charity worker, for heaven's sake, waited to go on a date with her man.

Not *her* man. Val. Valentino Vasquez. Her *client*.

"Pull yourself together, Amber. Do your job."

She'd kissed a handsome man. He'd wanted to kiss her. Had given her the option to refuse. Didn't mean they were going to make babies and live happily ever after. Sometimes two people kissed because they wanted to. They had sex because they wanted to.

"Sounds like a boring sex talk for teens," she muttered bleakly. Because she didn't get satisfaction from a hookup. It was so empty. She wanted more. She wanted that *duende* Val talked about.

She slid out of bed and paced the floor before the patio doors, which she'd left open all night, so blissful sleeping with a breeze dancing over her skin. She called Val and he answered on the first ring.

"*Buenos días*," he said. "Just waking?"

"You know it. Already deep into your code?"

"It's a living."

And what a profitable living. But also, a restrictive one when it came to occupying all the man's time. For heaven's sake, the man could retire. Never lift a finger amidst virtual code again!

"You know what I said about working so much."

"I know. I'll try to be home at a reasonable time today, honey."

She rolled her eyes at the endearment, while part of her melted at the intimacy of their jesting conversation. Handsome man giving her a pet name? It felt better than it should.

"I've great news for you." She leaned in the open patio doorway. "We've found a match for you. Ninety-two percent."

"That's…good. I suppose."

He *supposed*? What did he expect? A one hundred percent match? Ninety-two was incredible.

"So what happens next?" he asked.

No mention of their kiss. At least one of them could stick to business.

But was that all it had been to him? Kiss the girl. Back to business?

Amber closed her eyes and shook her head. She was a professional. She would proceed professionally from now on. No more kisses!

"Now we set up a date," she finally said. A patch of grass caught her eye. She looked down at her toes. "Her name is Carmen Alonso. She actually lives in Seville but she's leaving town in a few days so…how about tonight or tomorrow?"

"Tonight would be best. Wow. This is happening fast."

"It's what you wanted, right?"

"Of course." Was that a touch of reluctance in his tone? And why did that perk her up, give her a hope that she shouldn't even wish for?

"Do you have any questions about Carmen?"

"Should I have questions?"

Yes, he should. He should want to know everything about her. Where she was born, lived, went to school, what she did for a living, what she did in her free time. What her thoughts about dating were, what her thoughts about handsome billionaires were. If she were a gold digger.

"I will forward her profile to you, so you can take a look over it."

"Sure, I'll see if I can find some time to look it over. But I'm not worried. I trust the algorithms. Set something up for tonight."

"All right." He was being too indifferent about this. Like it didn't matter. Like it wasn't going to possibly be *the* date that could change his life. "Can you at least suggest a restaurant to meet at?"

"Let's do the Trastienda."

The same place he'd taken her. The food was excellent. The atmosphere perfect for a first date. Was it his MO? Had *she* been just another date?

You are not *his date! Ever!*

Amber stepped out onto the grass. "Got it. How about seven?"

"That works. Will you send me a text reminder?"

Seriously? "Val, I'm not going to be here to send you reminders for every meeting or date you have."

"I know. I really need an assistant. I wonder if Carmen has ever done any such work?"

"She's a recruiter for a global charity organization. Don't even ask her if she does secretarial work. That's very condescending."

"Right. Uh, I gotta fly on this job. Seven, then?"

"Yes, and do me a favor and arrive at the restaurant ten minutes early."

"I'll be home by six to change. See you later, honey."

He hung up and Amber could but only stare at her phone. He'd used *honey* again. Jokingly? Absently? What was wrong with him that he wasn't over the moon about a potential match? He had contacted Lux Love for this.

And why was she letting it bother her so much? If he messed up tonight's date, that was on him.

Well. It was on her. Colette insisted her consultants continue their work until they were assured the client had found *the one* and marriage seemed imminent. It didn't require staying near the client, but making sure a second date happened, and following up with those first two dates to get feedback was vital.

Which meant, if tonight's date went well, then Amber was out. So why did she feel as though this client was going to mess up majorly? That she might even need to fix his tie or adjust his hair, as if she were a mother making sure her offspring were presentable before he stepped out?

"He'll be fine."

Tonight, Val could meet his match.

And all the time they'd shared, the fun they'd had, the laughing, the conversations would be over.

She swore softly under her breath. She was jealous of Carmen Alonso. The woman might win Val!

And the only way to remedy that was to remove herself from this situation. Consultants rarely stayed on after dates began for their clients. Communication was continued through phone calls. And she was a consultant who did her job as expected.

Amber retrieved her suitcase from the closet.

The bull's head on the wall opposite his bed stared at him. He *had* told her she could put it anywhere. Was the placement her idea of a joke? Amber didn't do jokes. And it wasn't funny.

Eh. It was funny. He may get used to it there. Though, he couldn't stop associating it with his dad. Not conducive to a good sleep or even a sexy liaison.

"Amber!" Val called down the stairway and made his way toward the guest room. At Amber's suggestion he'd gone with a suit. Good first impression. He didn't mind the white business shirt. It wasn't starched so he'd keep the coat on to hide the wrinkles. But this tie!

Amber's head popped out from her room. She saw him dangling the tie and shook her head. "Come inside."

He splayed out his arms in defeat. "I never wear ties."

"Seriously?" Her red lips pursed—lips that he'd kissed—as she perused the situation then started folding one end of the silk tie over the other. "You've got quite a collection of them in your closet."

"They come with the suits. Or they are gifts from women."

"Really? So the women you date read suit-and-tie kind of guy from you?"

"Right?" He winced as she tugged the tie too tightly, which prompted her to loosen it. "But I am capable of change. Last night, I was Mr. Relaxation."

"That you were." She met his gaze, tilted her head as if searching for something, then focused back on the tie.

Was she thinking about that killer kiss they'd shared? The one he'd not stopped thinking about all day? Had even lost his way during coding and Hal had prompted him to pay attention. That had never happened before!

Why couldn't he have kisses like that all the time? And not from any woman. If Amber were among the potential matches on Lux Love's database, would they match?

"Have you ever used your service?" he asked as she adjusted his tie.

"What? Lux Love? As I've explained, we're not allowed. I'm no expert with ties, but I think that'll do." With a pat of her hand to declare the job finished, she stepped back and, hands on her hips, looked him over.

He did love that authoritative pose she assumed. Trying to look all in charge but her soft red lips and wavy hair always gave her away. She wasn't so sour on romance as she liked to believe. And he counted kissing as romance.

A smart guy could hack into the system and add her file to the database—no, he wasn't a hacker. Not that he couldn't do just that.

Amber hadn't taken her eyes from him. Val asked, "What do you think?"

"Handsome, talented young billionaire looking for love? Who wouldn't fall for you?"

Assuming his best leading man swagger, he asked, "Would you?"

"Well." Hand to her hip, she surveyed his attire. "We have been on a few dates already."

"Did you fall for me? I mean…" If she were to play this game, he could as well. "…purely in the sense of you doing your job, seeing if a potential match would fall for me."

"Of course." She ran a hand along the back of her neck, then quickly gestured with her palm between them. "Only in the sense that I was a stand-in for another woman."

But he wished she was not.

"Yes, I could see any woman falling for you. But most especially Carmen. I've read her profile. She's a lovely woman with good values and a successful career. A ninety-two percent match is very promising."

Val noticed her suitcase open on the end of the bed. "Are you packing?"

"Yes. I, uh…well, tonight's date could be the one. Beyond the follow-up interview in the morning, you don't need me anymore."

"Yes, I do." He rushed over and tugged the suitcase from under her touch. "I mean…" *Needy much?* "I haven't taken you to see the Metropol Parasol yet. Or there's a cool old cathedral by the bullring. And the beaches in Cadiz."

"Val, we don't need to do the fake dates anymore. Your profile is complete. Now all you have to do is let the algorithms do the work."

"Algorithms." For the first time, he almost hated that word. Because finding a match meant Amber would leave him. There would be no more world-rocking kisses. No more midnight movies under the moonlight. No more wondering if he might take her on a virtual adventure into an Egyptian pyramid. Or to Mars! They'd never gone on a jog together! No more… Amber.

Amber pushed her suitcase aside to sit on the end of the bed.

Val sat beside her. He eased at the tie to loosen it.

"Still too tight?"

"I feel so confined."

"You don't have to wear the tie."

"I want to—" *Impress Amber.* Because she'd suggested it would look good. "No. It's fine. I can suffer through one date with a noose around my neck."

"Please, do not go into your date with that thought to drag you down. Are you nervous?"

"Of course!"

"You've never seemed nervous around me."

"Because you're easy to be around." He twisted and pressed his forehead to hers. "You calm my chaos."

Her moving away from him actually hurt his heart. "You are chaotic," she said as she stood and fitted her hands to hips. "But it's who you are. Nothing wrong with that."

"Really?"

"Really. Initially, I thought you were too erratic, too busy to slow down and take notice of the world. Let alone a date. But I was wrong. Just be Val. That's the guy Carmen will love. Think of our dates as practice. Just pretend it's me you're talking to, if that'll help."

"Why can't it be you?"

Val suddenly felt as though he were back in school. The awkward geek who could never get a girl. If Pablo were still alive, he'd have slapped Val across the shoulder, winked and told him *Go get her.*

But the *her* in question was named Carmen.

He could do this. He *would* do this. At the very least, his dad would be pleased to hear he was making a concerted effort at finding his future wife. And who knew? He and Carmen may hit it off.

"I should head out. Will I see you later tonight?"

"I don't know, Val. What if you bring Carmen home with you tonight? It wouldn't look good to have another woman staying in the guest room."

He gaped at her. She intended to leave *tonight*? But more so… "I never do that on a first date. Sex on the first date is—you know that about me."

"I…did not. I just don't want to interfere in any manner. My boss would kill me if—"

If she what? Prevented him from seeing Carmen tonight? Actually let down her defenses and used her own advice to relax and enjoy their interactions?

She sighed. "Fine. One more day. I will need to do a follow-up interview with you in the morning. It's important."

"Fair enough. Then you have to stay. For the interview."

"Yes, for the interview. But if it goes well with Carmen, you must tell me. I reserve the right to leave you to romantic bliss with the woman of your dreams if that's what comes of tonight."

"Deal." He fist-bumped her, but he wished it was a kiss. "See you tomorrow morning."

"Good luck tonight!"

He paused in the doorway. He didn't need luck; he needed Amber in his arms.

CHAPTER THIRTEEN

ONE MORE DAY? Amber wanted another day with Val. Another chat. Another walk. Another kiss to end all kisses. Another movie night featuring them singing song lyrics at the tops of their lungs. Another standing in near darkness holding his virtual hand. He had caught her when she fell. It had been a storybook romantic moment that she hadn't known how to react to at the time, never having been a receiver of romantic gestures.

Was her dating life so terrible? Yes, it had been.

And why was that? Too picky. Too exacting. Expecting too much from the men she dated. Was her need for control stifling her reception to pleasure?

Her parents' divorce had affected her as well. But it shouldn't. That was between the two of them. She wasn't her mom or her dad. Why did she feel the need to blame her poor dating history on anything but her own shortcomings? Was she too focused on perfection? Even her mother had been able to set work aside and just be a mom when she had been home with Amber.

"I'm being too hard on my mom," she muttered. "She had her reasons for leaving the marriage. Reasons I shouldn't judge. I should give her a call."

She looked at her hand. Curved her fingers as if to hold Val's hand. He was smart, but he didn't wield that intellect as a front for his personality. It wasn't his label. He didn't label anything or anyone. He was his own man. Everyone around him was their own person. He saw everyone for however they wished to be seen.

And he saw her as pretty, smart and—kissable.

With Val, she didn't need to be perfect. She could be herself. And beyond the studiousness and quest for perfection, Amber was just a girl wanting to be loved. To be caught when she fell. To be kissed like the world was ending.

And the one man her heart had decided to pump for, she was sending out to meet another woman tonight.

"Ninety-two percent," she muttered. "Not the highest match."

Most of Lux Love's matches were 95 percent or higher. But as soon as the computer spit out a name above the 90 percent minimum, then it stopped its search until it was prompted to continue.

She picked up her phone and dialed Elise, who

worked evening hours at Lux Love because she had a morning job at a patisserie. Elise brought home so many expired baked goods; they were still good to eat, if a little dry.

"Amber! How's Spain?"

"Delicious in all the ways you can imagine."

"I know! Senor Vasquez is one delicious bite. I see we have a date scheduled for him tonight?"

"Yes, he left a while ago. Headed out to meet his future wife."

"Fingers crossed. Or…?"

From Elise's tone, Amber sensed she had caught on to the reason for Amber's call. Elise was the closest she had to a best friend. Though they saw one another at work, their free time together was rare. But in those spare moments, they managed to convey their likes, loves, hates and quests. And the girl code bonded them by a common love for all men with a sexy accent.

"You want me to check your numbers?" Elise whispered.

Amber panicked at her lowered voice. "Is Colette in the office?"

"No, I'm all alone."

"Whew! You scared me. But…yes. Would you? Just for kicks and giggles. You know."

"Of course. Kicks and giggles. Whatever that means. Hang on."

Elise was Swedish and she often gave Amber

the glazed-eye look whenever she used an American idiom.

"I'm running the stats. Want me to call you back as soon as I get results?"

That could take an hour.

"Yes, please?"

"Just for fun," Elise said. And Amber could almost hear her conspiratorial wink. "He is a sexy one."

"Too sexy. My reluctant heart is—oh, Elise, don't run the stats."

"Too late."

Amber knew it wasn't too late. All Elise had to do was execute the stop command. She was second-guessing herself. Knew this wasn't going to prove anything one way or another. If she and Val matched, then her heart could only break even more. And if they didn't match, then it would prove that Amber Martin would never find her man. Because she just couldn't loosen up and allow happincss to enter her life.

"Talk soon," Elise said and hung up.

Amber tossed her phone to the bed. It was early still but she wasn't in the mood for a walk. A shower would lift her spirits and then maybe a relaxing wander in the courtyard.

Carmen's smile was genuine and kind. Petite, blonde, very animated. Not overly gushy, but not shy either. She spoke with elocution and their initial handshake had been firm. A gorgeous woman; she would turn any man's head. The scent she wore was curious. Astringent with an undernote of floral. Val didn't like it, but he wouldn't say anything.

Throughout dinner they exchanged questions, volleying answers regarding work, hobbies, favorite entertainments. The usual. She didn't balk or wrinkle her nose when he drifted into the tech details about his work. Though she did wriggle in her chair when he mentioned his late work hours.

"I'm trying to change that," he added, as the waiter took away the empty bottle of red wine and replaced it with another. "I don't need to work as much but I do enjoy the purpose."

"Did you work today?" she asked.

"Every day but Sundays." Or most Sundays. He did try. Really, he did.

"You attend Mass?"

"When I remember. You?"

"Every Saturday evening and midweek if possible. It's important to me. But I'm willing to overlook your forgetfulness."

He shrugged and tilted back another swallow. "I don't want someone to view my worship schedule as lacking."

"I didn't mean it that way. Well… Faith is important to a healthy family environment."

He'd read that as he'd skimmed her profile. Didn't bother him. He'd grown up in a religious home and truly did wish to attend Mass more often. But…choices. His work was the most important thing in his life right now.

Save for finding someone with whom to share that busy life. Someone who didn't chastise him for it, even if she did like to suggest he work less.

Val smirked to himself. He didn't mind when Amber told him what to do. He understood it was a part of her perfectionist personality. The need for subtle control. Something that didn't bother him. Because she wasn't perfect and that made her even more appealing.

"After I marry, I intend to become a homemaker," Carmen said. "I love what I do with the charity aspect of my job. But raising children is a job in itself and I feel taking on the role of homemaker would be immensely satisfying."

While he was saddened she'd give up such an interesting jet-setting career, he also understood raising children was a job that should get overtime and vacation pay. "Good for you. I'm sure your husband will be very happy about that."

Carmen raised her wineglass and said, "To a happy husband in my future."

Val clinked his glass against hers. Yes, but… he wasn't going to be that husband.

* * *

Clad in a striped-linen pajama set, Amber had taken a blanket out to the courtyard along with a goblet of wine. Not the orange wine. That stuff was capable of making her walk into walls!

Alone but for the discordant chirp of a hidden insect, she drifted into reverie. Would Carmen find Val as charming as Amber did? The only thing Amber sensed might not vibe between the two of them was the religion aspect. Val didn't seem overly religious. Amber had been raised Catholic but considered herself lapsed. But she was open to attending a service on Val's arm.

"He's not yours to fit into your fantasies," she muttered and tugged up her legs, settling against the cushy back of the lounge chair. "He and Carmen are probably laughing over shared interests and drinking wine right now."

Pouting would get her nowhere. Nor was it a good look on her.

Her phone jingled. Amber hesitated answering, but ultimately couldn't resist. "Elise, are you *still* at work?"

"I like to burn the midnight oil. I take my laptop out to the terrace and watch the Eiffel Tower twinkle on the top of every hour. And I don't have to work tomorrow morning. So… I got your results."

"Yeah?" Her heart suddenly thundered. It was

just for fun. Really. But she and Val did have a lot in common. What if they matched in the nineties? "Tell me."

Elise's sigh did not bode well. "Sixty-two percent match between Amber Martin and Valentino Vasquez."

"Oh." Her heart suddenly quieted. Seemed to stop beating completely. She pressed a hand to her throat. Nodded.

"You okay, Amber?"

"Of course, I am. It was just a silly check. Right?"

"Right. But...*right*?"

Nothing at all felt right now.

"Amber, have you fallen in love with him? It can happen as quick as a blink."

She nodded. Then shook her head.

"Amber?"

"I—no, of course not. Don't be silly. This is my first consultation. I'm not so foolish as to jeopardize my job. Besides, Colette hired me because she judged me as too emotionless to ever match anyone. So make of that what you will."

"If you ask me, Colette is the emotionless one. She doesn't even notice Jacques pawing at her feet like a puppy."

The office took bets on how long Jacques could go until telling Colette he was in love with her.

"It's okay to lose your heart to the clients, Amber. It's happened to me."

"And what did you do?"

"He matched with a woman at ninety-five percent and they married three months later. That's what I did."

"But it hurt?"

"Of course, it did. Still does a little. He was so kind. Called me Sugarpop. So don't take this too hard. But also, don't be too hard on yourself."

"Thanks, Elise. I should go." Amber clicked off and set her phone far away on the bench where she had cuddled up under the orange tree.

She tugged the blanket up to her face to catch the teardrop that spilled down her cheek.

Val wandered into his home and strolled toward the inner courtyard where the solar lights beamed along the path to the stairs. Amber sat on a lounge chair, legs pulled up and a blanket around her shoulders.

A smile was irrepressible. She'd waited up for him? He liked having her face be the first thing he saw when he returned home.

She patted the chair beside her and he sat, loosening his tie. That felt great. A sniff tracked the astringent perfume Carmen had worn. She was still on him? He hadn't even gotten that close to her. Well, he'd kissed her cheeks in greeting and they'd hugged when parting.

"Makes me feel good to know that someone waits for my return home."

"Even after a date? Shouldn't that be the opposite? Like I was expecting your date to end poorly and—here you are. It's barely after midnight. What went wrong?"

"Is this the follow-up interview?"

She crossed her legs before her, assuming her take-charge mode. "Yes."

"All right. Nothing went wrong. Carmen was lovely. A beautiful person. We had a great conversation. We share many things in common."

Amber tapped her lower lip. "I sense there's a *but*."

He shrugged and leaned back, putting his feet up on the edge of a big terra-cotta pot, home to a massive palm. "I don't know. I didn't feel anything toward her. There was no spark. Her perfume was..."

"So strong." Amber winced. "It's all over you."

"Right? I'm going to have to send this suit to the dry cleaners. And when she said she intended to give up her career to become a homemaker once married, it hit me wrong."

"You don't want a wife to stay home with the children? I thought traditional was what you were shooting for?"

"Well, sure, but it was the idea of Carmen giving up a job that meant so much to her. Do you know she travels worldwide for charity?"

"I read that about her. Noble."

"It is. And I have nothing against stay-at-home parents. It just felt like such a loss to abandon the work that obviously gave her passion."

"How do you think she felt about you?"

"I think she liked me. But does it matter? I… don't want to see her again."

"Oh."

"I've failed my dad," he said. "But also, I've failed you."

"Not at all."

"But your algorithms…"

"Doesn't mean two clients are going to hit it off. We use a complex system to match people, meticulously examining all aspects of their lives. But there's a whole new level *beyond* the algorithms. Once you meet face-to-face and talk. The most important being will you match on a soul level?"

"Soul level?" He turned to face her. She wore striped pajamas that reminded him of summer and beach parties and not having a care in the world. He wanted that. "That's not something a computer can predict. Not unless you find a way to program it into the system. No. It's just not possible."

"Exactly. So the human element will always be necessary when it comes to matchmaking. And I mean—well, the soul level thing is not a part of the Lux Love litany so I shouldn't interject my own thoughts."

"Please do." He took her hand and kissed the back of it, studying her reaction. He could sense a flinch in the flex of her fingers but she didn't pull away. So he curled his hand about hers, holding it lightly but surely. Holding Amber's hand was so much nicer than holding Carmen's hand. And she smelled like everything that made him happy. "What does soul level mean to you?"

"I don't think a person can put it into words. Sort of like *duende*."

Exactly what he was thinking.

"It's a feeling," she said. "A knowing."

"Yes, a knowing. Like this person checks all the boxes and would make any guy a perfect match but…there's just that *something* that you can never fit into a tiny little box waiting for a check mark."

"The ineffable something," she agreed.

"Like the goose bumps."

She tilted a smile at him.

"That's the kind of love I want," he explained. "The kind that gives you goose bumps every time you see her because you know she's the one for you."

"That's a good way to put it." She smoothed her fingers over their clasped hands. "I'll inform the office to run the program to find you date number two."

"Thanks." He bowed his head over their hands and kissed her skin, lingering, inhaling as much of her as he dared. He wanted to keep the essence of her in his memory forever.

Amber shivered and he looked up as the breeze wafted her hair across her cheek. "I have to return to Paris tomorrow," she blurted out. With a gentle tug, she extricated her hand from his. "Once the client starts dating, my job isn't to babysit or linger."

What to say to that? This moment was so intimate. So easy. "I don't want you to go. I like spending time with you, Amber."

"Yes, well… Fraternizing with the paid consultant isn't getting you any closer to finding a match."

"Isn't it?" He stroked the hair from her face.

"Val. That's not…"

"Not what? How it works? Aren't you interested in me? Is there a rule against consultants dating their clients?" he asked.

"Of course there is."

"There shouldn't be." He touched the ends of her hair and twirled a bit around his forefinger.

"You're the most interesting person I've met, Amber. Ever."

"Well, that's…" Her sigh settled heavily in his chest. "Val. The algorithms were the very reason you called Lux Love. You trust a computer program to do its thing and to pick the perfect match for you. And, I only want what is best for you. So, don't make this any more difficult than it should be. I'm…going to bed. I'm sorry your date didn't work out tonight."

Her leg skimmed his arm as she rose and walked away from him. The sensation raised a wave of goose bumps on his forearms. And all Val could do was smile.

CHAPTER FOURTEEN

VAL PACED BEFORE the stuffed bull's head.

He wasn't sure how he was going to keep Amber in Seville. He was not ready for her to walk away from him. Algorithms or not. She wanted what was best for him? There was something between the two of them. And she felt it, too. But for some reason she was too afraid to admit to that shared feeling. Was it because of her job? Did she put that over him? As an employer, he would expect employee loyalty.

But as a man he wanted her to be real, to show him exactly how she felt about him. To kiss him with all her heart and soul.

They needed more time. He wanted to show her how he felt about her. Do more things with her. All the things. Spend every moment of every day with her. Holding her hand. Sitting quietly beside her—a feat for him, but so easy when in her presence. Kissing her silly. Do more than kiss her. He wanted to make love to her. He knew they would be perfect together in bed.

Yes, perfect. But could it be the perfection she strove to achieve? He should just out and ask her: *Do you like me?* That felt so juvenile. He wished Pablo were here to give him a shove and tell him to go for it. He should talk to Teo. Feel him out on what to do. They did have to discuss the ball, which was now less than a week away.

He wanted Amber at that ball, dancing with him.

"Val!"

He responded to Amber's call and ran down the inner courtyard staircase to meet her in the foyer. A wheeled suitcase rested near her leg. Already leaving? But he'd thought…

Why couldn't she wait until later? Or never?

"You're leaving so soon?"

She clutched the designer purse against her midsection and he noticed she was wearing the fancy suit she'd worn the first night they'd met. The consummate professional.

"I have to return to Paris. Colette has another job for me starting tomorrow."

"But what about…" Him? They hadn't done all the things. He hadn't told her what was brewing in his heart. His soul. About last night's goose bumps!

Was it so easy for her to walk away from him?

"Don't worry, I've got another match for you,"

she said. "And guess what? This one is a ninety-nine percent match."

"That's…" He didn't care about numbers or percentages. AI would never know his heart, or the way Amber made him want to jump and smile and shove all work aside. Screw the algorithms. He wanted her to stay. "…a lot," he said stiffly.

"Ninety-nine percent is almost unheard of. I've emailed her profile to you. I'm sure this woman will be your soul match. But we'll know more after the first-date follow-up."

He winced at the term *soul match*. He'd thought he'd found that already. *Duende*. But if Amber didn't see that, then he must have been mistaken. Still. She was leaving.

"The ball is in six days," he said. *Grab her! Kiss her!* "I'd like you to be there. To be a part of the celebration for all those we appreciate. I, uh, suppose I could set up my next date for that night. You'll want to see if the match is a success?"

Why had he said that? The last thing he wanted was for her to watch him match with another woman.

"I'll return for the ball if my schedule allows it. I'm sure Colette would appreciate me overseeing your date that could result in…a match."

She'd swallowed before saying that last part.

As difficult to say as it was for him to even think of matching with anyone other than Amber?

"Will you promise me a dance?"

"I…yes, I promise."

His heart thundered. He'd not lost her. Not yet. "You'll stay here, of course."

"Oh, I don't think that's wise."

"I insist. Maria will make up your room."

"My room," she whispered. Amber nodded and then— "There's something you should know, Val. I ran our profiles to see if we would match," she blurted out.

Val straightened, a smile growing. "You *are* interested in me."

"Well, I—" She backed away from him, hands going to her hips. "What I think about you doesn't matter."

"Why not?"

"Because we match at only 62 percent, Val. We are not meant to be a pair. The algorithms you put so much confidence in said so."

Val tugged her to him. She wasn't getting away with a simple handshake. His mouth met hers in a collision of sighs and thundering heartbeats. She initially pushed against his shoulder, but it wasn't with any force, no intention. A moan preceded her surrendering to the kiss. He spread his arm across her back, holding her from a fall from the pedestal he wanted to place her on. But only to sit there a while until she wished to jump down to do what made her happy. He expected nothing from her.

He wanted everything from her.

And he knew. That ineffable knowing. They matched on a soul level.

"Val! You said you trusted the algorithms."

"I do. I…did. Like you said, do we really want to put our trust in a computer? It doesn't know our hearts. Our souls."

A limo from the airport pulled up to collect her.

Amber touched his jaw. She smelled like orange blossoms. And something lost. *Duende*. When she walked away, he would lose that indescribable something that gave him so much joy.

"Don't leave?"

"I'll be back Saturday morning," she said. "If I don't leave now, I'll miss my flight. And my boss will wonder what's up."

"*What's up* is—"

She pressed her fingers to his mouth. "What's up is…" So many emotions fought on her face. He felt her frustration but couldn't understand her stubborn resistance to him. "I'm doing my job. And you need to accept that."

Val stepped away from her and shoved his hands in his pockets. Could he kidnap her and keep her forever? The desperate thought was not cool. But still?

"I've sent you the profile on your match."

"Right. The match." He'd gotten himself into this situation. A man should step up and face the facts. Perhaps the algorithms would find a woman who could fulfill his every desire. He'd never know until he gave it a go, eh?

His shoulders dropped. He didn't believe that for a single moment.

He waved as Amber slid into the back of the limo.

The one person who gave him joy was leaving him. Purposefully. She didn't want him? Or maybe it was that she didn't know how to accept less than perfect? Hadn't he tried to improve? To follow her suggestions of being neater, more generous with his time? He'd worn a tie, for heaven's sake!

No, those were surface things. What Amber desired was something that no man could match. Not unless she was the one to first unlock her heart and allow someone inside.

CHAPTER FIFTEEN

BEING BACK IN Paris should give a girl a big ole smile. Amber should feel like Emily strolling the streets in a fabulous designer outfit she couldn't possibly afford, so happy to have a job in the City of Love, and with oodles of Frenchmen to ooh and aah over. Not to mention the roommates in a tight little apartment in the 9th arrondissement to really bring it all together.

But Amber's smile hadn't returned since she'd driven away from Val's villa. She told him it was business. A lie. She had left behind that wonderful kiss. The man's hopeful wave.

She'd made a mistake. Because she'd had to for her job.

She didn't even believe in love! She'd never find it in real life. Why work for a place all about love? Not real love. Computer-generated love. They were merely matches. Didn't mean the people would click in real life. Find that certain something.

"Duende," she whispered.

Could she and Val have duende? She'd felt it. And while a few days in the man's life did not make for a lifelong connection, it had also felt like the beginning of something. If she set aside work. Which she could not do.

She could do that.

But…

"But why not?" she asked aloud as she walked down the sidewalk.

No decent reasons formed. And if she even thought to blame this on her parents' divorce, she'd have to kick herself. That was their life. Hers wasn't necessarily going to follow the same trajectory.

And while she had that thought in her head, she typed out a text to her mom: Thinking of you. Would love to talk. Can I call soon?

It was time to move forward.

Pausing again to check the directions on her phone, Amber leaned against the wall of a building. She had an appointment with Claude Lambert. He was in his seventies and looking for a woman his age to travel the world and go on adventures with. He'd already completed his survey and Amber now had to vet him. She didn't intend to stay overnight, as she had with Val. Perhaps cocktails at a nearby restaurant to begin his assessment. A date in the park would be an appropriate follow-up.

That may have been the first mistake she made with Val. Allowing the dates to blur the line between work and curiosity. So many other mistakes: overlooking his messiness, actually finding his distractions cute, making excuses for his lateness because he was a rich, important man. Not to mention, kissing him.

The final mistake had been walking away from him.

She'd see him again at the charity ball. She shouldn't go, but resisting the need to see him once again was impossible. One last look. One last conversation. One shared dance. Until…

He'd been matched at 99 percent. No way would that date not result in future dates. Soon enough, she'd probably see the Vasquezes on the wedding-gifts list that Colette kept for all her clients. And then there was the baby-gifts list.

Turning right, she crossed a cobblestone street and veered toward the centuries-old building owned by her client.

Val hadn't seemed too upset when she'd said she had to leave. So maybe what they'd shared had merely been a thing. Something that could have never grown to more. On the other hand, when she'd told him they'd only matched at 62 percent, he'd not seemed overly upset. He'd even asked if clients could date the consultants. He was interested in her. Damn it! This was so hard.

Could he care as much about her as she was beginning to realize she cared for him? Why had she allowed emotion into the mix? Amber Martin didn't do gushy romance and sighs. That was for all the other girls. The pretty, vapid women who judged others by their clothing, hair and nails. Amber didn't know how to relate to a man on a level that met her needs and desires…

She shook her head. No, that was an excuse. She wasn't emotionally stunted. And she'd had her share of romance before the divorce. And blaming it on her parents had reached its expiration date. She was too smart for that.

And with every touch from Val, she'd fallen a little further…

Don't fall in love.

"I haven't."

Who the hell was she kidding?

Valentino Vasquez was the only man she'd ever given a second glance to, enjoyed being around, thought about…constantly. But she had no intention of revealing that to Colette. In another month or so Val would vacate her constant thoughts and she would move forward, just as Elise had done that time she'd let her heart get in the way of her work. Vetting more clients. Moving up at Lux Love. Paying the bills. Following that career trajectory she had plotted so long ago.

What about your life trajectory?

Yes, what about it? Would she ever fit love into her trajectory? Was it necessary?

It was. A person couldn't live without an emotional connection. Feeling as though someone cared for them. Knowing they was loved. Thought about. Needed. Simply looking forward to spending time with another. That necessity had come to fruition this past week.

What if she dared to tell Val how she really felt about him?

Amber shook her head. No, that would not be fair to him. Or to his next match. Because it wasn't just about Val. Silvia Molina had paid for Lux Love's service and she expected results. Not to be told that the man she'd matched with had decided to take up with one of the consultants, too bad for you.

Arriving at the entry gate to the building's courtyard, Amber pressed the buzzer, and with a breath of confidence, entered when buzzed in. Today was about finding love for another client.

Val wandered back and forth on the holoplatform. He stood in a desert. A nearby camel snorted. Code scrolled around him and a checklist of the current projects stretched to waist level. He'd been in the dark room for hours and had gotten nothing done. He needed to verify his coders' work. And while he knew it would be flawless, he did want to browse the vibe.

Yet, every time he started to scroll through the code, he kept seeing Amber's face as she smiled at him while he performed on the restaurant patio. Or her silly way of putting her hands to her hips when she meant business. Or that soft glint in her eyes that he could never look away from. Brown eyes. Plain to some. But filled with such interest to him. When he spoke, she held eye contact and really listened to him. She wasn't waiting to reply as most people were wont. Had he ever experienced such rapt attention from a woman who wasn't set on winning his interest in order to finance her dreams of champagne and caviar?

With a tap of his finger, he selected the character-sketch program. A detail list appeared before him. He used this to create characters for Verdadero's games. "Hal, configure Amber Martin."

A hologram of Amber appeared before him. Hal used the camera and biodata to reconstruct her accurately. Stretching his fingers to widen the view, she grew to life-size standing before him. A trace of his finger along her head gave her curly dark hair a fluff. He selected eye color, making the brown more intense. The linen dress she wore was plain but soft and hugged her slender waist. If he put on the gloves, he could ask Hal to add in sensation. The feel of her hair would become soft and silken. Her skin…

Val dropped his hands to his side and stared at the hologram of a woman who had walked into his life and changed it in a way he hadn't expected. She hadn't asked him for anything. He didn't even know if she wanted a family. Children. A little house by the Mediterranean Sea? Or a glamorous mansion? It didn't matter. As long as they were together.

"Together," he whispered.

He smiled as his skin erupted with goose bumps.

CHAPTER SIXTEEN

Days later...

AMBER ENTERED THE final information for Claude in the database and leaned back in her chair at work. Already the AI populated possible matches for the client. All of them above 90 percent. Nice.

She glanced to her purse, tucked safely in the open desk drawer. Yesterday she'd spent some time shopping for a dress for the Verdadero ball. Hadn't found anything.

Or rather, she'd found plenty of options, a beautiful spaghetti strap number at a vintage shop that had fit her budget, but she hadn't been able to take the step of bringing it to the counter. Because that would mean she was okay with standing by and watching Val dance with his 99 percent match. Or on the other hand, perhaps Amber would be putting herself in the role of Cinderella, hoping Val noticed her instead of Silvia.

Ugh. She was so conflicted!

And her mom had finally answered her text this morning. She was traveling in Alaska—so many questions!—and would call Amber later today.

Amber looked forward to that call. Might she spill her heart to her mom and ask her advice? There had been a time when they were close and she could do just that.

"Claude texted me regarding your meeting the other day." Colette had a manner of appearing at her side. There were days Amber thought she had the ability to teleport. "He was impressed by your professionalism and kindness. Good going."

"Thank you. I always do my best." Unless the client kissed her. Many times. And made her fall—yet Val had caught her, hadn't he?

"We should have a few potential matches for him to select from before the day is over," Amber said. "And thank you for another client assignment. I know Chantelle comes back from maternity leave soon, so I—"

"Don't worry, Amber. You've been promoted to consultant. You'll receive commission on all matches you make."

Had she just…got a promotion? Delivered with the usual French manner of imperturbable disinterest.

"Thank you, Colette. I won't let Lux Love down."

"It's a trial basis, of course. I'll give you two

months to prove you've got what it takes. How is the Vasquez situation coming along?"

"Vasquez has another date in a couple of days. After going through the follow-up info on his first date, I feel certain it'll be a match this time."

Colette wobbled her head, neither agreeing nor disagreeing. "If it's not, do not worry too much. Some clients are fussy. I once had a client who went through a dozen women before he finally found the one."

"It's not a bad thing to be choosey when one is looking for a life mate." Especially when that mate was assigned by a computer.

"Yes, sure. I have another client for you." Colette tapped her pinging watch. She was always dashing off to lunch with clients and—from what Amber had learned through the office gossip mill—lovers. "He's in New York and will make himself available for an assessment."

"Oh." Another job so quickly? Yes! And yet. "I have a thing this weekend. Saturday, to be exact."

Colette tilted her head. With one look she could take in a person's motivations, life dreams and failures, Amber felt sure. She'd hired her because Amber was lacking in emotion? Not anymore!

"It's not necessary to be there until Monday, *chère*, but… I've never known you to have a *thing*. You don't do socializing. Certainly not *things*. What is it?"

To tell the truth? It was never easy lying and she wouldn't start with her boss. "Senor Vasquez invited me to the charity ball Verdadero holds every year. He was insistent. I didn't want to be rude."

"Is that the same event he's scheduled a date with the ninety-nine percent match?"

Amber would never accept the cold manner in which Colette called their clients by their match percentages. "It is."

"Hmm. That could prove to be an excellent opportunity for us to get some video for promotion. I'll send a cameraman."

"Really?" Colette did like to record events when she suspected an impending proposal. But for a first date? "Are you sure it's necessary?"

"Amber, this is the first ninety-nine percent match we've had in over a year. It can't fail. I might look into attending myself. Seville this time of year is just beginning to touch sultry. Do you think you can swing me an invite?"

"I, uh, can look into it." Yikes. Talk about turning her last chance to see Val into a promotional opportunity. "I'll check with Senor Vasquez."

"This Saturday, *oui*?"

"Yes, I'll send the details once I have them. I'm planning to fly in the evening before. The city was so beautiful, but I didn't get a chance to do some shopping, so…"

She waited for Colette to accept her made-up excuse, but Colette was already strolling toward her office, her slim hips sashaying. French women embodied casual and calm. They basically expected the whole world to love them. And the whole world did. To have such breezy confidence!

Amber turned back to her desk and saw Claude's first suggested match had registered at 97 percent. The older man had been charming, hilarious and open to any woman who loved to travel. Good for him. She would give him a call.

But first, she texted Val, asking about an invite for Colette. She didn't mention her boss's plus-one would come wielding a camera. Any confidentialities had already been agreed upon in the contract Val had signed, such as using photos for promotional use.

He texted back immediately. Good to hear from you! Yes, bring along your boss and anyone else. We have room! I can't wait to see you, Amber.

The three dots pulsed for a long time. And when she couldn't decide if he'd forgotten to sign off or was erasing what he was typing, finally an emoji of a man's face with a VR mask on it popped up.

Not as exciting as a heart, but what did she expect? She was the man's matchmaker. There was no room for little red hearts between the two of them.

She returned a thumbs-up emoji. Then shook her head and set her phone aside.

"You are an idiot," she muttered.

When she looked aside, Elise, whose desk was across the aisle from hers, nodded and shook her head as if she knew every detail of angst battling in Amber's heart right now.

Luis called to cancel tonight's dinner. Val had forgotten about it. Again. But he didn't say that. He pushed aside his work on the holo-screen and his dad's profile image showed in the center as he paced the holo-platform.

"Anything wrong, dad?"

"No, I just think with the ball this weekend that we could set aside the dinner. You know I'm not much for going out on the town."

That was a lie. The old man loved to hunker down in a bar and sing and chat with the regulars until the place closed. Did he not like the restaurants Val chose for their dinners? Four-star chefs were few and far between, but he always tried to impress his dad. Perhaps he was still angry Val had missed their last supper night?

The one that had plunged him into a quest for a match. And had fortuitously brought Amber into his life. He wouldn't tell his dad about her.

Luis Vasquez had a dislike for American tourists, all Americans in general. He viewed them as so materialistic! But he never tried to argue that one; his dad was set in his ways.

"I went on a date, Dad."

"You did?" A positive rise to his tone gave Val's shoulders a lift. "Tell me all about her."

He sat in the captain's chair and closed his eyes to his dad's profile image. "Teo turned me on to a dating service for professionals. She was kind and smart but…we didn't click."

"Oh." Positive tone? Evaporated.

"But I have another date the night of the ball. So…you'll get to meet her."

"I'm so excited for you, my son. Maybe she will be the one?"

"It's possible."

"My son is going to start a family!"

Val winced. Sure, he wanted to please his dad. But when Luis put it that way, it was almost as if he were filling an order for an insta-family. It was stunning to him that his dad, who had married for love, could be satisfied to see his son rush into a situation that might not be conducive to love.

"I only wish your mother was here to see the day her son walks down the aisle." *Lay it on thick, eh?*

"I wish the same," Val said. "But I take solace in knowing she's watching over me. Both of us.

Maybe you should use the dating service, Dad?" With a flick of his fingers, he brought up the Lux Love home page. "I'll swing for the profile on you. What do you say?"

"Your mother would not be happy to know I had moved on so quickly after her death."

Val shook his head. It had been thirteen years. "Okay, Dad, I won't mention it again."

"Maybe next year," Luis replied quickly.

Eh? So there was a spark of hope for his old man, after all. Val was happy with that. "Sounds good. I'll see you at the ball. Love you."

"I as well." His dad clicked off following his usual salutation.

Had his dad ever said the words *I love you* to Val? He couldn't recall him ever doing so. And to think about it, he'd not heard him say it to his mother. Luis was not emotionally demonstrative. It was the proud bullfighter in him. Any man who could bravely stand before thirteen hundred pounds of pure angry muscle would never show a soft heart.

And yet, there had been a few occasions, when Val was younger, that he'd spied his parents dancing or kissing as if they thought no one could see them. They had been madly in love.

Sometimes, actions were louder than words.

And the only action he'd been taking lately was following directions. Answering questions.

Making changes when Amber suggested. But he'd not stepped up and said—

"I want you," he said out loud.

And with a nod, he smiled.

CHAPTER SEVENTEEN

RETURNING TO VAL'S home felt odder than Amber had expected it would feel. Almost as if she were intruding, and yet at the same time, returning to a place she had always belonged.

She'd thought to knock and struggle with Maria's Spanish, and to be begrudgingly admitted entrance. But instead, Maria opened the door as she arrived, and gestured down the hallway toward her room as if it were genuinely her room. *Welcome back! We missed you!* Although the housekeeper didn't offer that verbal praise, she confirmed Val was working. To be expected. And since it was after seven in the evening, Amber thanked her and said she'd turn in early.

Ten minutes later, Maria brought in a tray of warm bread and herbed butter along with tea. A welcome surprise from the woman usually staunchly set on avoiding her.

Settling into a chair before the open patio doors, Amber inhaled, but the orange blossoms had all fallen and now the intense verdancy of the other plants and trees tickled her nose. The trickling fountain added a musical note.

Here in Val's home, Amber could stretch out and become a part of the space. Breath came easily. Life felt easy as well. The need to prove herself, to achieve and be successful, fell to the wayside. Anything was possible. Because Val made her feel welcome and seen. Like she was the only woman he did see.

So why had she walked away from him as if nothing had happened between them? And now to return to the scene of the crime and expect it to not be difficult?

"You really don't know how to do romance, woman."

Watching her parents as she grew up had been, she'd thought, a lesson in real and true love. Kisses in greeting at night when they returned home from work. Hugs for no reason but that they'd passed close to one another. That certain look thcy'd cast one another during movies as they related to something only they both understood. And always her dad had brought home flowers for her mom. Just because he loved her.

Dad was still pulling himself up after the divorce. But he'd asked Amber about her matchmaking service during her visit, so she'd taken hope he was thinking about putting himself back out there.

She checked her texts, and saw she'd missed a call from her mom while she'd been on the flight. Holding the phone to her chest, she nodded, then bravely hit the call button.

Amelia Martin answered right away. "Amber, I'm so glad you called me back. It's been too long since we've talked."

"Sorry I missed your call. I was on a flight to Seville."

"Your dad told me that Aunt Judy got you a job in Paris. How do you like it?"

"Dad told you that?"

"Well, yes, dear. We talk on occasion. Well… It's been about six months. I know he's taken this divorce hard so I try to allow him his space and to direct where he thinks our relationship should go."

Dad had not told Amber that when she'd visited. Interesting. So they had some secrets between them. And that was probably as it should be.

"I'm sorry for pulling away from you after the divorce, Mom. I, uh, was very mad at you."

"I know you are, Amber. And I'm sorry, too. But it is my life."

Was she like her mom? She didn't want to ultimately break a man's heart after twenty-five years of marriage. And yet, that wasn't a fair summation. Her mother was kind and loving.

Amber had witnessed the real love between her parents over the years. Of course, people changed!

"I'm beginning to understand that. I had a storybook ideal of my parents, and one of the pages got torn out. Maybe an entire chapter. But I'll survive. And…" Amber sighed. "Mom, I need to ask you something."

"I'm always here for you, Amber, despite the distance. Promise. So, what's up?"

"It's about a man."

"Oh. Do tell." Her mom's tone was curious with a hint of gossipy girlfriend, which gave Amber an infusion of hope.

Her mother *had* changed. Had grown out of love with her dad in the romantic manner. It wasn't for Amber to say that they should have soldiered on in a loveless marriage. It would have been worse for her dad to have remained with a woman who had fallen out of love with him. They'd earned their gold star for twenty-five years of devotion, and nothing could ever take that away from them.

So…okay. Love changed. But did that mean a girl should never allow herself the risk of love? That felt too constrictive. And not even smart.

"I'm afraid to let him in because—" she swallowed and lifted her chin "—because of you and Dad. How your marriage ended."

"Oh, sweetie. How will you ever know love if you don't allow someone in?"

"I know that. Rationally."

Would she ever take that first step? She couldn't think about the tangle of emotions that had brewed to a bubble since meeting Val. But Val didn't belong to her. He belonged to the woman he was meeting tomorrow night at the ball. Or, he could belong to her.

"How does he feel about you?"

"He's made it clear he is interested in me. But he's a client. For Lux Love. I'm supposed to be matching him to his perfect love."

"Well." Her mother paused for those few seconds she generally did before she announced wise thoughts. "Is it possible you already have found that match for him?"

Amber knew she alluded to *her* being his match. But before she could argue that it wasn't allowed for a consultant to fraternize with a client, she shook her head.

Here she sat, Amber Martin, not the biggest romantic in the world. Forever to remain unattached. Unless she got her act together and started paying attention to her needs. When would she step out of the shadows and show everyone who Amber Martin really was? What she really desired? What she could achieve?

She'd been trying to do that all her life. Rarely achieving the perfection she craved.

What was so great about perfection, anyway? Val had shown her that chaos could be kind of fun. Sexy and—had she actually tried to change him? To guide him toward being neater and working less? Nonsense! The man was perfect as he was. A beautiful mess, as the bartender had told her.

And some woman would be very lucky to call him her own.

Could that woman be her?

The urge to find out struck her. Hard. Glancing into her room, she noted the suitcase sat at the end of the bed. No ball gown inside. Would the shops still be open tonight? And if they were, might they be close to the Verdadera office tower?

"I think you know the answer," her mom said. "You're a smart woman, Amber. Always have been, always will be. You know what to do."

"I do," Amber said with new wonder. "Thanks, Mom. Can we…get together soon? If you're ever in Paris?"

"I'll make a point of planning a trip to France this summer. Love you."

"I love you, too, Mom."

"Amber!"

Val turned and leaped through a streaming waterfall of glowing green code to greet her. He caught her in a big hug. "I missed you!" A double-cheek kiss followed.

His words felt genuine. Amber didn't want to push out of his comfortable hug, and she would not. "Good to see you again."

"More than good. I'm excited that you're here."

He held her hands and looked her over. She hadn't changed in just under a week. But had he? His eyes were so liquid and dreamy; they possessed such depth. How had she not managed to stumble into them?

You already have.

"I'm so glad you decided to stop into the office."

"Well, I went out dress shopping but the stores were closed, so I thought I'd stop in and say hi since I figured you wouldn't return to your villa until well after I'd crashed." Totally preplanned, but he didn't need to know that.

He checked his watch. "Right. It is late. I should stop work."

"I don't want to bother you."

"Please. Bother me." He took her hand again. "I like the distraction of you."

Oh, was he ever a distraction. But her? She wanted to believe she could make a man forget about work simply because she was there, but… Maybe? Dare she believe in herself for once?

"Sorry. It's just… I know." He exhaled. "I'm acting like a lovestruck puppy dog."

"Oh, I wouldn't—" Lovestruck? About…her?

"Don't make excuses. Amber. We need to talk. Before the charity ball."

"About what?" Hands going to her hips, she asked, "Are you not pleased with Lux Love's services?"

"It's not that at all." A scruff of his hand through his hair distracted her from her innate need to put up a wall against connection. "Let's be real with one another. What we have between us has nothing to do with Lux Love. And you know it."

She did know it. She'd been unable to think of anything but that knowing since she'd gotten off the phone with her mom.

Val slid a hand along her cheek and cupped the back of her head. She knew the kiss was coming, and before she could plead with him not to make this more difficult, their lips crushed against one another. His thumb eased along her jaw, tilting her head to fit him more perfectly. All her doubts, her vacillations with whether to dive in with him, rattled against her rib cage, pleading for escape. To be forgotten or ignored.

Breaking the kiss, Val searched her eyes. "Don't tell me we shouldn't have done that. You have feelings for me, Amber, I know you do."

"It doesn't matter." Yes, it did! "It can't matter, Val."

"It matters to me."

"But Lux Love—" Difficult to put any belief in those strident objections anymore.

He kissed her again. His fingers stroked into her hair, trilling shivers across her skin. "Now that you're back in my arms, I want us to be honest with one another."

She had been honest. Getting involved with a client was a huge no-no. But that didn't make it wrong. And she might never know what could be possible if she didn't at least set aside those objections for the moment. For the night.

"For tonight," he said, "we're going to ignore the algorithms."

She had every notion what *ignore* meant to him.

He kissed her jaw and trailed more kisses down her neck. Shivers scattered over her skin and she recalled he'd said something about wanting goose bumps love. Mercy.

And she wasn't going to deny it anymore. This is what she wanted. Or at least, for the night.

She bracketed Val's head with her hands and kissed him. Hard. Taking what she wanted without apology. Aware they stood on the holoplatform where she had previously fallen from a cave wall and into his arms, she wondered if he could create a forest around them, or even a sandy white beach. But did it matter? They were alone. They both wanted one another. She wasn't going to let this chance slip through her fingers.

"Is Hal listening?"

"Uh… He's recording our biomarkers."

She swore.

"Hal, remove all data from the previous ten minutes."

"On it, Valentino."

"He calls you Valentino?" Sounded so personal. Did the man have a closer relationship with a computer than her? Time to change that. "Can you—" she took in the streaming green code around them "—turn him off for a while?"

With a wink, Val said, "Hal, go dark for two hours."

The code did not disappear, but she assumed the AI was not listening. Or hoped it was not.

"Two hours?" she asked, surprised at the generous timing.

"You need more time?"

She wanted all night. "No, that'll work."

She walked him backward toward the chair and when the backs of his legs hit it, he dropped into a sitting position. Amber leaned over him, placing her hands to either side of him on the chair arms. "You said something about creases in your boxers? I've developed a new appreciation for a messy man with a touch of perfection."

CHAPTER EIGHTEEN

THE FOLLOWING MORNING, Val did not miss the discerning eye Maria cast him while holding Amber's hand. He called to Maria that he'd be back in time to prepare for the ball. His housekeeper's gaze was drilled on the hand-holding. One of her eyebrows raised.

Val had no excuses. He and Amber had slipped in late last night and…she hadn't spent the night in the guest room. They'd had a thing last night and he was riding that thing into today. His emotions were jittering up, down, side to side, as if they were his physicality. But he couldn't control them by focusing on streaming code or going for a jog along the river. The only way to serve what he was feeling was to spend the day with Amber. To hold her hand. To enjoy the moments. Because in the back of his mind, he was very aware he was going to meet another woman tonight. And that what he and Amber had right now could very possibly be just Right Now.

He programmed his car to take her on a tour

of Triana, the old neighborhood where he grew up and would spend his weekends watching his mother dance on the back patio, showing him the steps and then allowing him to move as his body demanded. They cruised by the school where he and Teo and Pablo had been forced together through a tutoring program, only to become immediate and fast friends. The three musketeers!

His memories of Pablo were bittersweet. And with the ball tonight, he and Teo would once again honor their departed friend. Val knew Pablo would be proud of what they had accomplished.

Amber was curious about the massive network of wood that formed a mushroomlike canopy in the midst of the city, so Val took her to the top level of the Metropol Parasol, or the Las Setas, where they walked along the gangways. The view of the city was incredible. He pointed out the landmarks that held meaning for him, the Torre del Oro, a dodecagonal military watchtower that had stood since the thirteenth century; Royal Alcázar of Seville, the royal family's official residence surrounded by gorgeous gardens; and many historic cathedrals.

Amber spied the cathedral of Seville so they made that their next stop and climbed the tower Giralda. Val had seen it all and tended to dismiss most of the sights, and yet, seeing the architecture through Amber's eyes gave him a new perspective on his beloved city.

Allowing her to point and choose their path, he gleefully followed her from tourist trap to tourist trap. After stopping for lemonades, they decided to walk, hand in hand, for the short return to his villa.

"My father used to fight in the *bullring.*" Val pointed it out as they passed the Maestranza Bullring.

"The exterior is beautiful." Amber took in the baroque facade erected from stone and wood in the mid-eighteenth century. "Do you attend the bullfights?"

"On occasion. Do you want to attend one?"

"Absolutely not."

He got it. He'd learned long ago not to begin a controversial argument with someone who had not been born and raised in the land of bullfighters. The bulls were often killed. If not in the ring, then later in the stables. Wasn't as though an animal tortured with the picadors could survive or live through another fight.

On the other hand, some bulls showed such valor in the fight, exceptional bravery, that they might be pardoned. The indulto. They were retired to pasture or put out to stud and allowed to live a long life. Such as the bull whose head currently hung on his bedroom wall.

"But maybe..." Amber paused and looked across the street to the bullring building. "Doesn't look like anything is going on in there right now."

"There's not a fight this afternoon. They give tours when there are no fights."

"I might like to take a look around. Learn a little about what your father once did?"

"Really?" That was the most open he'd ever seen her and he was thrilled she was interested in his father's profession. "Just a quick tour, *sì*?"

She placed her hand in his. "Let's do it."

Amber learned a lot about the national pastime of bullfighting, but even after their casual stroll through the *facility*, she decided to stick with her revulsion for the sport, though she didn't say that to Val and he didn't press her for a new and positive impression of it, either. She appreciated that about him. He never seemed to nudge her toward his beliefs or to change to suit something he preferred. It really brought her first week here with him to a fine—and poking—point. She had tried to change him. Fool.

But she'd only had his best interests in mind. And she still did.

Now they strolled along the Guadalquivir, hand in hand. Spending time with Val was more valuable than any metaphorical gold star Amber had ever earned.

"You and your father… You'd like to be closer, yes?"

Val exhaled. "We are close and we are not. There will always be a chasm between us because of my career choice. And he was never pleased about my friendship with Teo."

"Oh?"

"Teo's family… His dad was involved in criminal activity. Teo has been fighting that stigma all his life. And as you've likely surmised, my dad is very judgmental."

"Maybe he wants the best for his son. And knowing one way of life, I'm sure it's difficult for him to embrace you stepping so far out of the traditional realm of careers. Though, I must say, bullfighter doesn't scream *traditional job* to me."

Val laughed but then admonished with a waggle of his finger. "If you were a Spaniard, you would not say such a thing."

"Fair enough. Do you ever wonder what your life might have been like if you had chosen dancing?"

"Let's see…" He stepped ahead of her a few paces and snapped his body into a pose, arm up and chest proud. "I'd be a world-famous flamenco dancer who travels the world and brings duende to the masses." A few rapid taps of his feet ended in a splay of his hands and a bow. Accompanied by a self-effacing laugh.

There was nothing funny about his talent. Every movement he made, whether comical or sensual, captivated her. "Yes, duende. I'm starting to understand that word."

"Something untamable, soulful, yet also understood once you allow it to step inside your life."

"Is it a little…sexual, too?"

"Yes. In certain moods, of course." He took her hand, swinging it, then pulled her in for a kiss. The trace of his fingers along the back of her neck put her right back in bed, lying naked beside him, breaths gasping. "I know watching a performance can turn people on." The way he gazed at her should be labeled a sexual move, as well. "Even dancing, if you let go of your inhibitions, can be a turn-on." He laughed. "I like sex. Good old-fashioned sex. Uh, just in case that was a question for your notes."

"Likes sex? Dully noted."

Val leaned in closer. "What about you?"

"Me?"

"Did you…like what we did last night? And this morning?"

"I love sex." *With him. Tell him only with him!*

He pulled her along the sidewalk, turning to face her as they slowly walked. "But if you don't have romance?"

"Romance isn't required for sex," she answered

by rote. *No, don't spoil it!* Why couldn't she just be real and tell him her truth? That she was so into him and wanted him and—

"That's sad."

"That's not—"

"I thought we were really into one another, Amber. But there's a part of you that isn't willing to get fully on board. So what we had, at least in your eyes, wasn't duende."

"Like you said, duende is an ineffable thing, so hard to truly explain."

Val shaded his eyes with a hand. "Duende is the way music and art makes you feel. Right here." He gestured a cupping motion over his heart. "A euphoric but knowledgeable state of abandonment. It can only be felt through true, deep immersion in the craft. It's like an orgasm. A real one that only comes from true connection. Once felt, you want more of it."

"Val, let's, uh…" She walked ahead of him, splaying out her hands. "Can we just enjoy the walk?"

Because if she did hand him her heart on her palms, then he'd have to return it. Tonight. Before his date! It wasn't fair. But she didn't know how to stop the script and alter the ending.

He rubbed his jaw, noticed the ping on his watch. He glanced at it but didn't answer the call.

"You can get that," she said. "I'll walk ahead."

"No." He rushed up to join her. "It's just my dad. I'm sure he's checking on the time for tonight's event. He does that when there's important meetings or when he used to have a fight. Needs to second-check everything. I'll introduce you to him tonight but do allow his evil eye to zoom right over the top of your head."

Amber laughed. "Much like the stink eye we got from Maria before leaving?"

"She cares about me but would never step in to express an opinion. She shows her respect and love in the things she does for me. I'm not going to mention to her that I've looked into a house cleaner."

"You did? That's wonderful. But I understand. You don't want to step on Maria's territory."

"Not even that. It's just… I'm comfortable the way I am. Do you really think I need to change for a woman? Why can't we accept one another as is? I thought that was the purpose of the vetting. If I change, then I'm not me. I won't match the profile."

Amber winced. "I do like the beautiful mess you are."

"You do?"

She squeezed his hand. "Oh, my gosh." She grabbed Val's wrist and checked his watch. "We've got to get back to your place. The ball."

"We'll head back. But first, I have to say something."

"What is it?"

"Last night wasn't just a one-night fling for me."

"Oh, I…" He was going to say it. And she wasn't prepared to deal with the truth at this moment. "But your date is tonight. It's been scheduled for days."

"I know, and I would never cancel on Silvia at the last minute."

"And you should not. This is what you wanted, Val." It was what she had initially wanted, to be commended for her matchmaking skills. Everything had changed. "For Lux Love to pair you with someone."

Did she still require that gold star for a job well done? That little piece of gold foil could never patch the hole she already felt in her heart.

"Maybe they have already achieved that goal."

Her mom had said the same. So why did a small part of her still resist the inevitable?

Val bowed his forehead to hers. "Set aside the fact that I've a date tonight. If that wasn't in the cards, how do you feel about me?"

"I do care about you, Val."

He kissed her forehead, then swept down for a quick brush of his lips against hers. "Shouldn't have done that," he muttered. "But so glad I did."

"Same. But..." She exhaled.

Val nodded. Put his arm around her shoulders. "I get it. You've got a job to do. Let's get back to the villa. Life...is waiting to wobble us both tonight."

CHAPTER NINETEEN

AMBER LEFT VAL to run up to his room and change while she sat in the kitchen sorting through her emails. Colette had sent her a text before boarding her flight in Paris. She would be in Seville soon.

The realization that she'd forgotten to buy a dress while they were out sightseeing didn't bother her. She didn't intend to go to the ball now. How could she stand and watch Val fall in love with another woman? A woman selected specifically for him to be his perfect match?

It wasn't fair. And she wasn't going to further bruise her heart watching them come together. She'd make an excuse to Colette that she wasn't feeling well. And she'd tell Val that she intended to arrive later because she had some last-minute work to finish.

So what if they'd made love last night…and this morning? And so what if she was getting vibes from Val that he was interested in her. They weren't a match. 62 percent!

"You're not ready!"

Amber turned to find her goofy billionaire CEO had transformed into a suave, sexy charmer dressed in a tuxedo with a glint of diamonds at his cuffs. Even his shirt was black. His dark eyes brooded from beneath a sweep of curly raven hair.

A big smile overtook her face even as her chest tightened. Another kiss was all she could think about. And sex. Lots of sex with this man. All day. Every day. With code streaming around them. Without the code. Just. Sex.

"Duende," she whispered to herself.

"We forgot to buy you a dress," he said.

Happiness? Yes, this man did make her happy.

"Don't worry about it." She summoned a quick lie. "I ordered one online. It'll be here in an hour."

"Perfect, but I am needed before the ball kicks into gear…"

"You go ahead. I don't want to arrive with you anyway."

"Why not?" Had he ever looked so puppy-dog sad before? So kicked?

"Val."

He thought about it. Rubbed a hand over his face and shook his head. "I get it. Might look suspicious to—what's her name again?"

"Silvia Molina. Her family owns a cacao farm

and she co-owns a marketing firm with her best friend."

"Right. I read about the chocolate. I've never much liked chocolate. And… I'd prefer arriving with you on my arm."

"Well, that's not going to happen. One of us has to maintain a modicum of propriety."

The look he gave her said everything she was thinking. *Why the propriety? Because we want to grab each other and make out, be damned everyone else?*

"Do you have a tie?" she asked. "Or better yet, a bow tie. I think that would look great."

"In my closet." He gestured over his shoulder as Maria walked in and started to coo over her employer's handsome good looks.

"I'll run up and get one for you," Amber said, slipping from the kitchen. "I know where to find it!"

She skipped up the inner courtyard stairs. Putting distance between herself and Val was foremost. He was so… Mr. Right. Standing there and *not* touching him would have been impossible.

But that's all he was. Right in her heart right now. She was infatuated with him. Still riding the sex high. And after an afternoon of walking hand in hand as they'd done the tourist thing, she knew she was riding some kind of romance buzz that would eventually settle to a simmer when she realized they were not a good match.

She veered down the closet hallway and eyed the tie rack. A black bow tie would get lost against his all-black outfit, but maybe the silver one? Yes, very festive. Grabbing it, she strolled back down the hallway and—

It wasn't locked. It was ajar, as she'd purposefully left it. But she couldn't put her hand to the knob to pull it open. She stepped backward, and once back in the main closet, she sat on the chaise and pressed the tie between her hands.

"What am I doing? How did you end up here, Amber Martin?"

Sitting in a billionaire's closet, getting ready to send him off on a date that could prove to be with the woman he got goose bumps for. They would date, get engaged, marry, have children and live happily ever after. Valentino Vasquez would get exactly what he'd paid for. She would have proved herself to Colette that she could see the matchmaking process from start to finish. Life trajectory? Right on course.

So why did she not want to bring this bow tie to Val? The niggling feeling that she could sabotage this evening *in some way* startled her. She wasn't that person. Okay, a little. But he hadn't said he hated the bull's head in his room, so there was that.

But Val wasn't just any man. Even now, she wondered if he'd rush up the stairs in search of her having possibly gotten locked in the closet again. He'd find her. And kiss her again. And every day to follow.

Such intimacy certainly did not fit into her trajectory of moving up at Lux Love, making more money, paying off her bills and finding her own place to live.

Why couldn't she have all of that, including the intimacy? The love? She and Val had moved beyond consultant and client. And she didn't want to struggle with the wrong of that anymore. They'd made love because they were two adults who could do as they pleased and didn't have to answer to anyone about their desires.

But the part of her that strived for perfection still wouldn't allow whatever wanted to happen to happen.

Even if she lost the best thing that had entered her life?

Val swaggered in to find her sitting on the chaise. Without lifting her head, she held up the bow tie for him. If she looked into his eyes, she might— Holding back tears made her wince.

So when he knelt on the floor before her and slid his hands along her thighs, her body pleaded for her to fall against him, to hug against his *aza-*

har scent and let the tears fall. Yet her innate stubbornness insisted she resist.

"I think you and my closet have something weird going on," he said softly.

She laughed but then sniffled.

"Amber?" He touched her cheek. Always touching her. His love language. "Why the tears?"

Yes, why the tears? She'd come to terms with the fact she couldn't have what she wanted. But could she tell him that? *Did* he want her? Was she more than just a one-night fling to him? He'd told her he cared about her. But he couldn't if he was going to meet Silvia tonight. Val was not the sort of man who would go on a date out of obligation. Maybe?

"I think I'm overwhelmed by this job, actually. It's gone quite well. I'm happy for you," she forced herself to say. "Tonight could change your life."

"My life has already changed since meeting you."

"Don't say that."

He tilted her chin up and held her so she couldn't look away. "I will say it. You're the best thing that's ever happened to me, Amber. I'm not going to deny it."

"It's not even been a week that we've known one another."

"How much time does a person need to know here?" He patted his chest, right over his heart. With a heavy sigh, he shook his head. "I won't argue if you insist this is just a job for you. But know, I wish it was you I will be dancing with tonight."

"We can still have one dance." *If* she went to the ball. Which she did not intend to do. So, more lies? Oh, Amber! "It's probably best if I stay away."

He pulled her into a hug. It was a comfy, all-encompassing embrace that surrounded her with his scent, his being. His soul.

Her soul knew this moment was right. But she didn't feel goose bumps.

"Please come to the ball," he whispered in her ear. "Give me that dance. I don't want to be there unless you are."

A lot to put on her shoulders. Tonight, the man should only be focused on meeting and getting to know his match.

"I'll need your nod of approval," he said, pulling out of the hug. "If you like her, then…nod?"

Really? Did he not know her heart?

No. Because she'd not dared tell him how she felt about him.

Because… Amber Martin was not as perfect as she vied to be. And if she was going to match Val to his perfect partner, then it couldn't be her.

Amber nodded. She took the bow tie from him and clipped it to his collar. "You're going to do great tonight. And when you meet Silvia, use your friend Pablo's wise teachings to impress her."

"I don't want to impress her. I want someone with whom I can be myself."

She wanted the same. "I get you, Val. You *are* yourself. Smart, fun, a little erratic. It's when you get into your head and start thinking too much you lose the natural rhythm of you. Just…be Valentino Vasquez. Geeky CEO and all-around nice guy. She'll love that guy." Because Amber loved him. Damn her heart. "You'd better go. You are the host."

He stood and helped her to stand. She daren't ask for what she wanted from him. It wasn't what a professional would do.

"Come as soon as the dress is delivered?" he asked.

She nodded. "Of coursc."

"Then I'll see you later." He leaned in, as if to kiss her, stared at her a moment, then redirected his mouth toward her cheek. A soft flutter of a kiss landed at the edge of her eye. Not enough. But already too much. "Promise you'll come."

"I…" Amber sighed against his cheek. She gripped his lapel. Then stepped back from him and nodded. "Yep. See you later."

As he walked down the long hallway, she caught a hand against her throat.

If she fell in love with every client, this job was going to wrench out her heart and smash it against the ground.

Just like now.

Half an hour later, Amber turned off her phone because she'd gotten a text from Colette. Her boss was en route from the airport and would be an hour or more until she got to the party. How was it going?

She wouldn't lie to her boss, so it was easier to avoid texting that she wasn't even there.

Humming preceded Maria's entrance into the kitchen. The housekeeper strolled to the fridge, grabbed the handle, then did a double take on Amber sitting at the table. "You are not at party?"

Amber turned her own double take on Maria. "You can speak English?"

The woman waggled her shoulders gaily and nodded her head. "Why you are not at party? Valentino wants you there!"

"I know that." But why the sudden switch to English? Had she understood Amber's English all this time? What might she have said that she shouldn't have said in front of Maria? Unbelievable! "I can't go. I…don't have a dress."

"Oh, no, no, no." Waggling a finger at her, Maria approached Amber. "You go."

"I can't. I..."

"I know." Maria patted her heart with a palm. "I know."

"You know...what?"

"That you are in love with Senor Vasquez."

"Oh, I'm—"

Maria shoved Amber's shoulder—not so lightly—to indicate she get out of the chair. "Come with me. Come!"

Amber followed, but only because she was in shock from learning the maid could speak English and that she obviously thought she knew something that wasn't true.

Lying to herself again?

"It's necessity," she muttered as they passed the guest bedroom door and reached the end of the hallway where Maria's room was. "What do you want, Maria?"

"I have dress for you. Come."

"Oh, I couldn't."

The woman was going to lend her a dress? She was a foot shorter than Amber and carried a good thirty pounds more than her. And really. What would she possibly have that Amber could wear?

Not that she was considering going to the ball. She'd made that decision. She had to stick to it.

Right?

The housekeeper disappeared into a closet, so Amber lingered by the door. The room was sparsely decorated with a bed, a dresser and chair, and a cross on the wall. A pretty floral motif danced around the window that overlooked the outer courtyard. It added some happiness to the plain room. Did Val not treat his hired help better?

No, she knew that Maria would want for nothing more. He'd offered to buy her a big-screen TV to watch her stories and she'd refused. The older generation did like to stick with their comfort items.

Maria emerged from the closet with a stunning red dress on a hanger and displayed it proudly before Amber.

"That's gorgeous." Amber took in the low-cut neckline and spaghetti straps and narrow waist. The skirt blossomed out in layers like a flamenco *bata de cola* and was decorated with floral embroidery much like the painted design hugging the window. "Where did you get this?"

"I wore it long time ago. I could not part with it. Too precious."

"Oh, then I can't…"

Maria held it up to Amber's body. It seemed the perfect length and size. "I was once like you," Maria said. "Slender. Not so much on the hips. It will fit you. You take."

"No, you said it is precious to you."

"I want you to wear it. It only collects dust otherwise."

Amber touched the soft fabric. *Magical* came to mind. And something a princess might wear.

"And put up your hair. I will help. Hurry! You must go to the ball!"

"I'm not sure."

Maria pressed the dress into Amber's hands and said, "You love him."

Amber shook her head adamantly. How could she possibly know?

"I know. You are good for him."

"Do you think so? Maria, you've never been so—" What did it matter? It was too late! "Val is going to meet his perfect match tonight."

"Eh." Maria made a dismissive gesture. "You? Not perfect. But just right, I think."

Why had the woman never said that to her before? Had she said anything to Val? Likely not.

It felt like a fairy-tale moment. The fairy godmother handing the plain and romantically misfit Cinderella a fabulous gown and telling her to show up at the ball where the handsome prince sought his match.

Maria leaned in, a smile glinting in her dark eyes. She tilted her head and asked plainly, "Do you dare?"

Amber held up the dress, knowing it would fit.

It was everything she was not. Everything she thought she wasn't.

Why not slip into a new and more authentic skin? One that wasn't so set on perfection? One that sought duende over algorithms? Tonight, she wanted to walk into the ball and dance with her prince.

"Just one dance."

CHAPTER TWENTY

SILVIA MOLINA WAS PERFECT. Beautiful, well-spoken, graceful, smart, engaging and she was even a bit of a geek. As the CEO of a marketing management company, she focused on connecting influencers to their key sponsor targets; she was steering the business toward great success.

From Silvia's profile Val learned that they shared a lot of interests. VR gaming? Check. Surfing and snorkeling? Check? Even old movies? Check. She smiled and listened intently when he spoke. Laughed when appropriate. And she pulled out a few flamenco moves as they swished around the dance floor.

So when Teo pulled him aside to ask him why he looked so bored, Val could only but scan the ballroom one more time—not finding who he was looking for—and shrug. "Not bored. Just…"

"She's beautiful."

"Yes, she is," he muttered as visions of Amber surfaced in his thoughts. He shook his head, jarring himself back to the conversation. "Oh? Uh.

Right. Yes, Silvia is pretty. Very accomplished. She's going to hit her first billion in a few years if she stays on track with her company."

"A successful woman is perfect for you."

There was that word again. *Perfect.* Val had heard it bandied about so much of late it had ceased to hold meaning for him. Or rather, it implied too much. A final result he felt sure he did not want to touch.

"Where's Cara?"

"She's getting something to drink." Teo, looking like a corporate raider in his tuxedo, nodded to a passing partygoer. Always keeping up the good will with their contributors. "Will you introduce us to Silvia?"

"Of course. You gotta trust the algorithms, right?"

Teo turned a concerned look at him. "What's up, Val? I sense you're putting on a front. And I know you're all about the algorithms, but really? Should a guy put such blind faith in ones and zeros when it comes to love?"

Teo nailed it. Of course, one shouldn't. Not after spending time with Amber and learning he'd like to spend the rest of his life with her. Sixty-two percent? That meant nothing. Computers couldn't factor in the emotional. The duende.

"Look at me and Cara," Teo said. "I don't think a computer could have ever predicted we'd stumble into one another's lives again and find love. Be careful tonight, Val. Use that brain that's made Verdadero billions."

"I think it's my brain that's gotten me in this mess."

"You could be right about that." Teo thumped Val over the chest. "Then use this. Your heart will never lead you in the wrong direction."

Val put an arm around his friend's shoulders and when he turned to take in the ballroom, all that he and his friend had accomplished, his eyes landed on the woman standing at the top of the ballroom staircase.

His heart double-pulsed.

Dressed in a body-hugging red gown that splayed out below the hips in a soft hush of ruffles and roses, she was unaware of his stare. Her dark hair was pulled up and red roses were tucked within it like some kind of flamenco goddess.

And her lips. So red. More roses. Her mouth last night as he'd held her naked body close and kissed every inch of it beneath the streams of code. Sighs had guided him to the best places on her skin. And when he'd brought her to orgasm, she'd startled, grasping his face and confessing it had never felt like *that* before. So good. Same for him.

She had lied to him about it meaning nothing.

So why was he here on a date with Silvia? What an idiot! If he never saw Amber again, he was the only one to blame.

Amber looked over the ballroom. Trying to find him?

Please, let it be me.

On the other hand, he'd asked her to nod if she approved of Silvia. He didn't want to see that nod.

Teo said something but Val didn't hear the words. A new yet intriguing rhythm took control of his heart. A symphonic duende pattered out steps that gave him a feeling of…knowing.

He turned his hand over to see the hairs on the back of it had risen.

"Goose bumps."

"What's that?" Teo asked.

Suddenly, Amber's eyes locked with his. A small curve of her red lips. Acknowledging him but not wanting anyone to notice? Cool and collected then. Just here to oversee the work she had done for her job? To ensure Lux Love made another successful match?

Val didn't want to be ad copy for the company's success rate. He wanted so much more. He wanted her to know about his goose bumps.

"I'll catch you in a bit," he said, leaving his friend behind as he made a beeline toward the goddess in red. "Amber," he whispered before he was close enough for her to hear. And when he stood before her, he took her hand and kissed the back of it.

She tugged sharply from his grasp. "What are you doing?"

Lost in the compelling draw of the one woman—the only woman—he could see, he'd forgotten his reason for this evening. *To find a partner. To please your dad. To make everyone happy.* But him.

Clearing his throat, Val said, "Sorry. You look like a bouquet of roses. So beautiful. I couldn't resist."

"Val," she said on a breathy gasp. Then, seeming to check herself, her propped her hands to hips. "Where is Silvia?" She made show of looking around. "I hope she didn't see that."

Val scanned the ballroom packed with Pablo Pascal Foundation contributors all glammed up to honor Pablo's vision that had rocketed Verdadero to the top. Pablo, the guy who had taught Val how to be cool around girls. He wasn't doing such a good job of it right now.

"She's over there in the white dress," Val muttered, trying to keep his gaze from the formfitting gown Amber wore. It was as though it had been tailored specifically for her. And he knew every inch of her body. Intimately.

How could she make love with him last night

and then, less than twenty-four hours later, act as though it didn't even matter?

"This is the dress you ordered online?"

"No, Maria lent me this dress. It's hers."

"*My* housekeeper?" He nodded. "Yes, she was once a *cantaora*. I imagine she entranced many a man wearing this gown. You wear it well."

"Thank you. I feel like a princess, that's for sure."

"I was thinking the same."

A shy bow of her head was so out of character for his precise and get-the-job-done lifestyle consultant. But then, Val felt out of sorts, too. He didn't know how to act, especially when the room was packed with people who knew him. Amber was just as nervous as him. Their lovemaking had meant something to her. It had to.

"Do you, uh—" her gaze flittered about the ballroom "—want to introduce me to Silvia?"

No. "Yes, of course, I should do that. But first, didn't you promise me a dance?" He hooked an arm for her to take.

Amber stared at his arm for a moment too long. Val's heart dropped to his stomach. "Amber," he said on an achy tone. The goose bumps tingled to alert again.

"Yes, that dance. Just one then." She took his arm.

Why did it feel as though he were forcing her

to walk alongside him? He'd never felt so conflicted about being with Amber. She walked stiffly, glancing everywhere but at him. And when they stopped on the dance floor and he faced her, taking her hands, she looked aside as they began to step to the music.

Had he lost her before he'd not even won her?

The song lyrics for "Quizas, Quizas, Quizas" said everything Amber had been thinking about Valentino Vasquez lately. *You won't admit you love me. If you can't make your mind up, we'll never, get started. I don't want to wind up, broken-hearted.*

How she wanted to speak those words to him. Ask him if he really loved her.

Tell him that she loved him. Because, yes, she did. And this dance before the eyes of so many strangers was torture.

Yet at the same time, she had come here to ensure he and Silvia got along. This was the best thing for Val. The algorithms he believed in confirmed it.

Perhaps? *Perhaps, perhaps.* She had to stop listening to the lyrics.

When they turned in a slow spin, and Val stepped close enough that their faces were but a breath apart, she glanced to the side. Because to look into his eyes would tear out her heart.

"So..." Conversation. Yes, talk to him. About

anything but her feelings. This was the last time she'd see him. Best to act professional. "How do you like Silvia?"

His mouth tightened. Annoyed by the question? *Take a number!* She was annoyed that her life trajectory seemed to be intruding on something that felt so…perfect.

"Silvia is everything a man could ever want," he finally said.

"Oh." Amber checked herself. The lackluster response was uncalled for. *Put on your business tone, woman! You're doing what is right for Val!* "That's great."

"Sure. She's perfect."

"But I thought you didn't want perfect," she said before she could edit herself.

"Everyone keeps telling me I need a perfect match," Val said matter-of-factly. "So. There you go. I got one. Thanks to you."

"Thanks to me." Her heart dropped, as did her voice. Difficult to speak more lies.

The song ended and a livelier tune began. Amber looked to Val for a sign he wanted to continue dancing but he was looking elsewhere. For Silvia? Of course, a 99 percent match.

What had she expected from their final dance together? That he would confess he loved her—always had? Always would?

"Val, what's wrong? You seem tense."

He stepped back from her, shaking his head. "You're a sham."

"What?"

"It's true. You're all about romance and finding happily-ever-after." Modifying his tone, he glanced around before focusing back on her. "But you don't even believe in it."

"Val, you've known that from the start. But maybe…" So much had changed since meeting him. Her ideas on romance and love especially. "I do believe in love. Mostly."

"No, you don't. You don't even care about this job. You just took it so you could move to Paris."

"Well, sure, but—romance and happily-ever-after is Lux Love's motto, not mine. We guarantee a match, but just because a computer puts two people together doesn't mean they are going to love one another. Love is the sham, Val, not me."

Val gaped at her. "Not what I expected to hear from someone I'm paying good money to hook me up."

"*Is* it just a hook up? You don't seem even slightly interested in getting to know your date."

"Because the only person in this entire room who matters to me…" He gestured between them, then, frustrated, flung his arm back. "You don't get it!"

Oh, she got it. Perfection-seeking Amber Martin had finally pulled down her wall. Her perfect life trajectory had collapsed. And she didn't know how to face that. "I can't do this."

Amber stepped away from Val and pushed through the crowd, seeking escape. A quiet hiding spot. Away from all the laughter and chatty conversation. Away from the touch of the one man who had made her believe that love could be more than just a sham.

Val started after Amber but didn't gain more than a few steps. From out of nowhere Silvia appeared with her mother alongside her. Both women had golden wavy hair, glossy nails and shiny pink lips. Immaculately styled. Designed to please the eye.

He tugged at his bow tie. "Silvia. Sorry, I was… That woman was with Lux Love."

"I know," Silvia said. "Mateo pointed her out to me. I was told by my consultant that there would be a representative from Lux Love here tonight. I'm sure the service needs to ensure they've done a good job. We want photos with our families! Come along."

She tugged his hand and he followed her weaving path.

A photo opportunity was the last thing Val wished for when a glance over his shoulder revealed Amber fleeing the ballroom like Cinderella trying to beat the midnight chime.

CHAPTER TWENTY-ONE

THE STAIRS LEADING from the ballroom were carpeted in red. Amber made it halfway down, then decided to sit on the side of the vast, curved expanse and lean against the stone wall. The lighting strung above the entry steps was magical and she could even go so far as to label it fairy-talesque. But fairy tales ended happily. Hers, having only just begun, never had a chance beyond those first few pages. The villain wasn't even Silvia. If anyone was to blame for her lacking happiness, it was Amber Martin.

She wrapped her arms around her legs and settled her chin on her knees. This fabulous dress had bolstered her confidence even as she'd tried to remain impassive to her attraction to Val. Dashing away from Val's embrace had felt necessary. She was only doing what was right for him. Silvia was his 99 percent match!

Amber should be happy for Val. For the fact that her first field assignment had gone well. Of course, there would be the first-date follow-up interview that must take place within a day or two. She could do that by phone. It would be too difficult if she had to face him.

Val had called Silvia perfect. But there had been no excitement in that statement. And Amber had to agree. More and more she was feeling less certain that perfection even existed. And if it could be achieved? Then what were the rewards but an even bigger and more arduous quest? Or the ultimate letdown of divorce? Was she doing the right thing by promising love to her clients? What if it was all just a terrible fantasy?

Might she ever be happy with not-quite-perfect?

Who was she to believe she deserved perfect? Maybe it was only reserved for the best of the best, the top one percent, the…

Amber shook her head. Perfection wasn't a prize for only the best and the smartest. It might even be less than desirable, as Val had said to her. What was wrong with a little chaos scrambled up in her perfection?

A beautiful mess. Yes, he was. And Amber didn't want to change a thing about him.

A man paused on the same step she sat on. She hadn't been introduced to him yet, but when she'd found a few moments alone with Teo, he'd pointed out Luis Vasquez, Val's dad.

"Senor Vasquez?"

Luis tilted his head. She stood and offered her hand. "Amber Martin. I'm the lifestyle consultant with Lux Love who arranged for your son to meet Silvia tonight."

"Ah, Senorita Martin, thank you." He shook her hand vigorously as his reserved attitude took on a warmer front. He possessed the same curly dark hair as his son, and a build that made her wonder if he also jogged to keep in shape. "I wasn't so sure about those fancy dating services, but I do believe my son has met his match tonight. She is lovely. And her family has lived in Seville for centuries. I knew one of her father's cousins. A bullfighter like myself."

Of course, he must be pleased that the family was as traditional as his. Make that as traditional as he desired. Val was the furthest from that expectation. Yet his blend of classic and modern viewpoints made him even more captivating.

Amber grimaced, unable to muster hopeful words for Val and Silvia's future—a future she couldn't bear to imagine. *She* belonged in Val's life. Not Silvia.

"I have never seen Val smile so much," Luis said.

Was that so? Amber had seen him smile when he'd first noticed her standing at the top of the stairs, and while they been dancing. But that smile had dropped once they'd started arguing about her support of romance being a sham. He'd been right. And then Silvia had arrived to whisk him off to take photos with her entire family. Who invited their family along to their first date? Val had to feel squeamish about that.

On the other hand, his dad was here. Those traditional values were strong. Not so dissimilar from her own family. Until they had crashed into a wall and altered Amber's idea of what romance should be. They'd not done it to hurt her, or to change her outlook on love. Amber Martin was her own woman. It was time to start acting that way.

"Val only wants to please you," she said. "He's doing this because he wants you to believe he's happy."

"Having a family will make my son happy."

"Yes, and I know Val wants that. But he shouldn't be forced into it."

Luis gave her a long side-eye. "What makes you believe my son is being forced? He is the one who contacted your service. And Silvia is perfect."

That word again. Val said he didn't want perfect. What had changed his mind? Beyond the fact that since Amber had arrived in his home, that's all she had promised him: The perfect match. Well, she could hardly discount that the man had gotten his money's worth.

"I shouldn't have made it sound as though he

was being forced," she said to his dad. "Val did contact Lux Love. I just…well, they'll have to date and get to know one another to see if it will ultimately be a match. Tonight can hardly be considered a date. They'll need to talk in private."

"Eh." Luis gestured dismissively. "Some families still arrange marriages for their children. It is a way of life you Americans cannot understand."

"Were you married to a woman you didn't know?" Though she knew the answer, she couldn't help but prod the hive.

"Of course not. Sophia and I… We were so in love. We dated in secret. My family was angry when I told them I was going to marry Sophia."

"Why?"

Luis shrugged and bowed his head. His body language softened and she sensed he was stepping into memories that must be difficult since his wife was no longer with him. "Sophia was a woman from Andalusia. Not good enough for the Vasquezes. According to my father."

"I get the family traditions and wanting to live up to accepted ways, but it is the twenty-first century. And your son may have stepped further into the future than either of us can comprehend. Val is a genius. He's creating new technology that will have a tremendous impact on more than gaming. You are aware of the educational games Verdadero makes exclusively for schools?"

"Sure, it is a good thing. I wish he could have found a way to make dance work."

"He is an incredible dancer." He'd danced his way into her heart. "I think he might start working toward fitting that into his life."

Luis regarded her with new interest. "What makes you believe that?"

"I made the suggestion that he shouldn't abandon something that gives him such joy."

"*You* said that to my son?"

"Well, yes." Had that been an accusation or disbelief? "Val is passionate about flamenco. As passionate as he is about his job at Verdadero. There's no reason he can't have both."

Luis looked her up and down. Assessing. "You are American?"

She nodded. Straightened and put a hand to her hip. "Expatriate living in Paris."

The old man grunted. She couldn't determine if it was positive or negative. "My Valentino is a good boy."

"Yes, a good *man*. Val is creating an amazing life for himself and he wants to bring in someone he loves to share that life. But as well, I sense he really wants to spend more time with you."

"I love my son. We disagree on many things. But… I am pleased you've put the idea of dancing back into his head."

She held up her fist for him to bump but he

stared at it. Wrong generation. She dropped her hand. "I should call a cab."

"The rideshares stop every so often. Just wait a few minutes and one will arrive. I must return to the party. Good evening, Senorita."

Amber caught her head in her palms. She'd made a mistake. Again. She didn't want perfection. She wanted the beautiful mess of a man she'd successfully pushed away.

So many photos. Val had been directed to hold Silvia in his arms for a few of them. Awkward. He didn't want this. Their first date should have been private. So they could talk without her family hanging on every word. But he knew the privacy wouldn't change anything. Ninety-nine percent match or not, Val was only interested in one woman. And it was time to talk to her. Without any dancing around the issue. So he'd escaped for some fresh air.

"Dad!" Luis Vasquez turned around at the top of the inner stairway as Val rushed up them. "Are you having a good evening, Dad?"

"I am, my son. The entertainment is remarkable. How were you able to get the Spanish Dance Troupe to perform?"

"Eh. Money can buy worthwhile things. Have you seen Amber? The Lux Love consultant?"

His dad looked him over curiously. "Why do you ask?"

"I need to say some things to her."

"You can say thank you through the service, *sì*?"

"Dad." Val exhaled and then placed a palm on Luis's shoulder. "I care about Amber. She's the first woman who really gets me."

Luis nodded. "Yes, she told me she suggested you try to fit dance into your schedule."

"You spoke to her? Where?"

"Do you really think that American woman is more interesting than Senorita Molina? Val, her family is wealthy and has lived in Spain for centuries."

Val took his dad's hands between them. "The Molinas are a fine family. As is Silvia."

"Then why are you looking for the American?"

He wasn't going to have this argument. They were too alike, yet very different. And both would have to accept that. "Same reason you defied your family's wishes and married my mother."

Luis nodded, bowed his head. "I do understand."

"Do you?"

Luis gestured over his shoulder. "Senorita Martin is out on the front stairway. If you don't hurry, she will be gone."

Val hugged his dad. "Gracias!" He raced toward the doors.

CHAPTER TWENTY-TWO

"AMBER!"

Amber swiped at a tear as Val skipped down the steps to her. He took her hands and looked her over as if she'd barely missed being knocked flat by a speeding car.

"Why are you out here? Why did you run away from me? Amber?"

"Val, you shouldn't be away from your party. I… I don't know what to say to you to make you understand."

"Tell me what's in your heart."

If only! "I can't."

"Why not? Are you afraid around me? I thought we were good together."

"We are. But I don't want to ruin things for Silvia."

"Ruin them!" He bracketed her face with his hands and kissed her. Deeply. Quickly. But there was no question he meant that kiss. "I just met her, Amber. It's not like one night is going to seal the deal and we're going to sign a marriage contract. We haven't even dated!"

"But you will. You have to if you want to get to know her better."

"I already know her. I've read her profile—she matches exactly. Perfection on paper."

Perfection. Ugh. Amber looked aside. "I guess you changed your mind about not wanting perfection."

"I didn't change my mind. I still don't want perfect."

"But…?" She peered over his shoulder toward the entrance doors. Somewhere inside stood the woman she had paired with the man who…didn't want perfection?

"All you have to do is say I mean something to you, Amber. That's all I want to hear."

"You do mean something to me. But, Val, the algorithms for us only match at sixty-two percent."

"Screw the algorithms!"

She gaped at him.

"I mean it! I want beauty and grace," Val said. "And intellect and laughter. But I also want crying in my closet and singing old show tunes at the tops of our lungs. I want perfectly imperfect, Amber. And that is you. Amber, I—"

"Amber!"

Both turned at the sound of a Frenchwoman's voice.

"Colette." Amber's heart dropped to her gut. "My boss."

Had Val been about to tell her he loved her? He wanted imperfect? Well, here she stood. Forever on a quest for perfect, but sadly, never able to touch it.

No. It was not sad. Amber Martin was not perfect. And she was very good with that.

"Senor Vasquez." Colette, shadowed by a fawning Jacques, wore a simple black sheath gown, heavily laden with diamonds. The epitome of French chic, she strode up the steps and stopped to kiss both of Val's cheeks. "I've come to see how satisfied you are with Lux Love's matchmaking."

"I…couldn't be happier," Val said.

Amber jerked a look his way. But he'd just said…

"I'm so pleased." Colette gestured toward the top of the stairs. "If you'll show me inside you can introduce me to her. Jacques, start filming."

"But you already know her."

Colette glanced to Amber. A perfectly arched brow lifted in question as Jacques zoomed in on the reaction.

"Amber is the match for me," Val stated.

"What?" Colette couldn't compute those

words. Her flawless veneer screwed up in confusion.

With a slide of his hand across Amber's back, Val pulled her in. "I love you, Amber."

He…loved her? Of course, she'd known he had feelings for her. Had tried to resist— "Yes," she said as a sigh. "Yes, I love you, too."

And in the next breath she decided to break all her rules and kick aside her trajectory and take exactly what she desired. She kissed Val. Not quick, but a long, deep, *claiming* kiss. One that told him without doubt that she wanted him. It didn't matter that Jacques was recording it. Or that Colette was gasping in shock. Amber's entire life changed in this moment.

And it felt like duende.

With a kiss to the edge of her mouth, Val paused and looked to Colette. The woman pressed a hand to her heart, unaccepting.

Back to that claiming. Never had Amber kissed someone as a means to…show off, but that didn't matter to her right now. What did was that Val had just spoken his heart. And it matched hers. She was in this kiss for the long ride.

She heard Colette mutter, "No, this is not happening again! Not another consultant falling in love with a client. There goes my ninety-eight percent. It's going to drop to ninety-seven now. Jacques, I need air."

"We are standing outside," Jacques said.

"Would you stop recording?"

"Yes, Madame. Shall I get you a martini?"

Amber smirked against Val's kiss, but she didn't break it, because—no, not foolish. Very smart. And completely in love.

"Get me a vodka," Colette grumbled. As her boss stomped up the stairs she called back to Amber, "You are fired, Amber Martin!"

Val stopped the kiss. His eyes danced with hers. Wondering if everything was okay. Did she need to run after her boss and smooth things over?

Amber directed the man back to her mouth to continue the kiss. She'd worry about the angry boss later. Right now, this Cinderella had won her prince. And whatever her life trajectory transformed into, it would be so much better now that she'd tweaked the algorithms to include Valentino Vasquez.

EPILOGUE

TWO MONTHS LATER, Amber officially moved in with Val. She hadn't returned to Lux Love. Her roommates had been thrilled to hear the gossip about Amber's daring—albeit unplanned—mutiny from the company. And what a reason to do so! She'd found her prince. A beautiful mess of a prince.

Now they stood in the dark room which had been transformed to the dusty red surface of the planet Mars. VR visor in place, and the gloves on her hands, Amber walked forward, exploring. Dust from her footsteps rose when she looked down, and just ahead walked Val in clunky moon boots and exploration gear.

They'd done it. He'd taken her to Mars, as he'd wanted to do. And though Val had wanted her to move in immediately, she'd wanted to honor her rent agreement, which was up last month. She'd spent that time looking for a legal research job online and had found one possibility, but ultimately hadn't wanted to move back to the States.

Or away from Val. She was still looking for work, but wasn't in a rush since Val wouldn't allow her to pay rent or any of the expenses.

When Val had promised he'd cut back on his work hours, he'd meant it. He'd cut that time in half. Which meant all that free time was spent with her. They'd toured the city, traveled the Mediterranean coast in his driverless car. She'd started taking flamenco dance classes. And she and Maria had developed a new connection when Amber had expressed an interest in learning about her stories.

Val's dad, Luis, had been over for dinner a few times and he was slowly getting used to Amber. She wasn't going to push. But she had made her mom's famous chocolate chip cookies for him one evening and he hadn't stopped raving. So there was hope for him yet to side with her.

Ultimately, Amber realized that she was a romantic at heart. But allowing a computer to match two people just wasn't her vibe. Maybe doing research for writers would be a thing? It would allow her to stay home and yet still do the work that gave her pride and validation. Val wanted her to do whatever made her happy.

And that was making love with him. All the time. Even under the watchful gaze of the bull's stare. Heck, she'd found a man who could stand before the bull for her. And always with a glint to his eye and a tousle of his hair. And creased boxers. Val was her beautiful mess. Together, their life trajectory would embrace chaos with a side of neat to keep it in balance.

"You see that dune just ahead?" Val asked.

"Yes. Do you want to race there?"

"Nope." Val turned in the game and his avatar smiled at her. "I don't ever want you too far from my side, lover." He held out his hand, and she took it. In the game.

And in real life.

* * * * *

If you missed the previous story in the Cinderellas in Seville duet, then check out CEO's Spanish Fling *by Justine Lewis*

And if you enjoyed this story, check out these other great reads from Michele Renae

Reunion with Her Highland Rival
Jet-Set Nights with Her Enemy
Billion-Dollar Nights in the Castle

All available now!